PENGUIN BOOKS

# ALL THAT IS OURS

Naadhira has been writing since she was fifteen and has never stopped. She spends most of her time getting sucked into books and daydreaming about fictional characters. She's a lover of words and languages and aspires to make all her dreams come true, specifically to publish all her stories.

*Indecipherable* is her big debut as an author—a self-published collection of poetry and short stories. *Our Tethered Skates* is her first fiction book, followed by the sequel, *Our Tethered Worlds*.

She can also be found on Bookstagram, Twitter, and Blog at @legenbooksdary.

# All That Is Ours

Naadhira Zahari

PENGUIN BOOKS
An imprint of Penguin Random House

PENGUIN BOOKS

Penguin Books is an imprint of the Penguin Random House group of companies whose addresses can be found at global.penguinrandomhouse.com

Published by Penguin Random House SEA Pte Ltd
40 Penjuru Lane, #03-12, Block 2
Singapore 609216

First published in Penguin Books by Penguin Random House SEA 2025



10 9 8 7 6 5 4 3 2 1



ISBN 9789815295481

Typeset in Baskerville BT, Ink Free by MAP Systems, Bangalore, India



www.penguin.sg

*To that Form 4, Maths Paper 2 exam,*
*where this story first came alive*

# PART I

# Chapter 1

'Aeni, wake up!'

Ma's booming voice awakes me as her knuckle repeatedly bangs on my bedroom door. Even in my barely conscious state, I can hear her footsteps as she enters the room.

Her brown hair, whose colour is highlighted when sunlight hits it, tickles my face. I slightly open my eyes, but it is more like a squint, trying to make out my surroundings against the bright sunlight pouring in through the windows.

Slowly, I open my eyes, and I can clearly see my ma standing beside my bed, her expression telling me to get up before I get a serious scolding. Even in the early morning, my ma looks fresh and, ultimately, ready to begin the day. At this ungodly hour, she is already up and about, doing a million chores around the house while I'm still in bed and the rest of the population of Killen is probably still in deep slumber.

I don't often see women Ma's age have the same hair length as her. She once told me that having long hair is something she'll never change—and I know the reason for this is my father. It must be painful for her to talk about my father, who really liked her with her long hair cascading down her back. On certain occasions, when she is in the mood to talk more about the mystery that is my father, my mind imagines how he must have been like and how our lives would have been today if he still was here with us.

Ma's luscious hair is not the only enchanting thing about her. Her beautiful features have also made men ask for her hand in marriage, and she has always refused them. She constantly says that it will be just me and her, no one else.

'Come on, Puteri Aeni! You do not want to be late,' she leaves the room, finally leaving me in peace.

I lie on my back and stare up at the wall in a daze.

In that moment, an announcement can be heard on the speakers that are connected to the domiciles across the city. The government broadcasts reminders or political updates over them from time to time.

'Attention, residents of Killen! It is a brand new day with a lot of possibilities awaiting you. Have a good day.'

As long as I have lived, I've only heard the same woman's voice from the speakers, announcing daily reminders and nothing else.

I'm getting a headache trying to get my mind to work at full speed this early in the morning. I dress up for a day at the Academy. Well, six hours of the day to be precise.

I grab a carton of milk from the fridge and pour it into a cup. I sit on a chair at our dining table, watching Ma heat up our breakfast while humming in her melodious voice. I find her voice calming, no matter how hectic my morning may be. I'm not always a morning person. Sometimes, I refuse to wake up for as long as possible, finally getting out of bed with just enough time to rush out the door and head out.

I take a sip of water, 'What's for breakfast this morning, Ma?'

'It's the usual for today. *Roti canai* with a side of curry,' even though she's not looking at me, I can tell that she's saying it with a small smile on her face because, for her and for me too, even the smallest things in our ordinary lives can be the best things.

I hum in excitement, 'Can't wait. It smells amazing already.'

'I'm almost done,' she tastes the curry using a spoon and momentarily glances at me, 'Can you grab the plates and bowls for me?'

'Yes, ma'am,' I stand up and make my way towards the lower part of the cupboards to the left side of the kitchen where we store them.

I grab two plates and two bowls, and hand them to Ma, who just turned the stove off, 'Here you go, my lady.'

'Thank you, darling.'

The smile on Ma's face never leaves her face and the sight truly makes my heart glow with love and reminds me how much I adore her. Since it's just the two of us in this single-storey domicile—number

53—that my parents were placed in when they got married, she is everything to me and vice versa.

Ma places the plates in front of our chairs, and we dig into our meal. The food isn't made from scratch. Each domicile is provided with meals depending on the total number of people living in them. Ma only heats the meals up so that they do not taste too bland as she has said countless times before.

It isn't wrong to prepare our own meals from scratch, and with the ingredients we have, Ma does it sometimes. But most people like us don't really like the hassle of cooking. It is why the slogan 'Precooked meals are the way to go' fits so perfectly with both of our preferences.

'Aren't you running a bit late?' Ma asks as she dips a piece of roti canai into the curry and looks at me.

'I still have a few more minutes to spare. Don't worry about it.'

She sighs, 'You can't act too cool about it. Your education is important for your future. Always remember that, Aeni.'

'Of course, I do.' I glance behind me, towards the living room at the clock. I really will be running late if I don't move now. Maybe very late.

I finish my breakfast, gulp down the remainder of my cup of milk, and wash the dirty dishes in the sink with much urgency.

I kiss Ma on her right cheek and say, 'I have to get going now. Bye, Ma!'

I sling my rucksack, which I placed on the sofa the day before, on my right shoulder, and as I open the front door, I hear her voice coming from the kitchen, 'I told you to not be late. Have a lovely day, darling!'

No one can argue that a mother's gut is always right. Always.

* * *

I briskly walk towards the tram station, my initial anxiety getting alleviated when I see the tram pull into the station. *Right on time.* I line up behind an old man who is walking with a cane, and I heave a sigh of relief.

Inside the tram, people from all walks of life, young and old alike, are crowded together. Some are heading to the Academy, others are heading to work while still others are going to finish off whatever they are to do out there in the city. As the woman from the speaker would say, it is a brand new day with endless possibilities awaiting us. I snicker at my own sarcasm.

A little girl with pigtails who is sitting beside her mother stares at me. Seriously, what is her problem? I stare right back at her as if we're in a staring competition. Not long after, I hear an announcement on the speakers that the tram is approaching Academy station. As it comes to a complete stop, I give the girl the most haunting look I can muster and leave right before I can see her reaction. The look on her face would have been priceless and worth it, but I'd really rather not have her mother scolding or giving me a dirty look. Right before the door closes, I hear a little girl sobbing, and I assume it is her. So far, my morning is off to a pretty good start.

The Academy is situated in the heart of Killen. It takes me five minutes to walk from my housing area to the nearest tram station, where I take the tram to get here.

The citizens' modes of transportation are extremely limited. There are only two options: take the tram or walk. Even though the tram is the only way of transportation around the city, it doesn't get crowded, as it is highly systematized. Every five minutes, a tram comes, regardless of what time it is or which station you're getting on from.

Arriving in front of the already opened golden gate with the rest of the students, I make my way inside the Academy.

The entirety of the third floor, which is the highest storey, houses the Elementary students. The little ones are no older than six years old and shrieks of laughter are a constant on their floor, especially during their breaks.

The floor below it is for the Primary group, our resident pre-teens who are eager for their turn to enter the teens' Secondary group, who are on the first floor. As for us Tertiary students—or, like the other students prefer to call us, the 'oldies'—two lower, basement floors are dedicated to us.

While the first basement floor is for the classes and cafeteria, the one below it is for our workspaces, where we spend the latter half of our days to practice our skills and get ready for the life after the Academy, also known as the working life.

The Academy has its own technique and system on how things work. Our learning programme falls into four distinct groups.

Group A, the group everyone looks up to the most. It consists of individuals who are most likely to run in the highest hierarchy of society. Like the officers working for the government, judges who yield to the law, and most sought out of all are the ones carefully chosen to work closely for the Permaisuri at the castle.

Group B contributes to our nation the most. They are soldiers and army officers who fight for our rights and independence.

Group C are the ones who work in the infirmary. Ma and Faye are part of this group.

Group D are the people who work in stores and information centres, where they work as administrators in an office or any other place that requires their assistance.

Lastly, we have the often-shunned Group E in which I have ended up. This is the group that makes food, clothes, or other things that can be manufactured. This group is considered the lowest of all. Truth be told, I personally think there is nothing wrong in working for this group, but society has a different opinion.

I quickly make my way down the stairs, a floor below the ground, which houses the office, teacher's lounge, and other special rooms for detention.

I rush to my classroom and am thankful that it is not situated at the end of the hallway. The building is enormous, and if you don't know where you're going, you seriously can get lost.

I don't stop at the door and head straight for my seat. I'm breathing heavily, which is probably wrecking the aura for the people closest to me. I'm just glad the teacher hasn't come in yet.

My friends—my only three close friends—greet me.

'Late again, Aeni?' Nihal teases.

'Shut up, Nihal. Give the girl a break,' Faye backs me up.

'But what I said was right. Only stating the obvious, unfortunately.' Nihal retorts.

Faye rolls her eyes, and they continue their morning banter. It's like their caffeine, as though they cannot keep away from it.

'Oh, Faye. Did someone wake up on the wrong side of the bed or is this a case of lady syndrome?'

'I'm sorry, but do you have something against women to be saying something like that?' She warns him.

In return, Nihal playfully acts like he's offended by her actions and starts complaining about rude people.

'So, Aeni. Is there anything interesting that I should be aware of happening in your household?' asks Indra, my third friend in our socially awkward group.

'Is this your idea of small talk? Because if it is, let me tell you that it's not and will never not be weird.' I give him an amused look because the way he asks me is way out of the ordinary.

'Whatever—'

He doesn't continue his sentence, as the teacher finally makes an appearance and drops a stack of her books onto the table with a loud bang. Since today is Monday, it'll be a fun day learning about our national language.

Even Nihal and Faye have stopped bickering and are already facing forward where our language teacher, Mrs Ruya, is standing.

'Shall we begin the class? We have a lot to cover today,' Mrs Ruya asks even when she knows no one will even be bothered to respond. Her monotonous voice makes it hard for me to stay awake. I bet, at this moment, the majority of the students are not even in this classroom, focusing on the teacher in front of them. I'm sure some are already drifting away to sleep or to wherever their imagination takes them.

'Today, we will be studying about the important usage of expressions—'

I lay my chin on the table and stare ahead as I, too, drift away.

# Chapter 2

'That is all for today's class. Thank you for your cooperation. I will see all of you next week. You are dismissed,' Mrs Ruya finally announces, and I snap out of a trance from wherever my mind wandered off. Who knew two hours could feel like a whole day?

We have an hour's break for lunch. Later, we will head to our own workspace to prepare food for the city. This way, we get hands-on training for our assigned work. After graduation, we do that work for the rest of our lives. Honestly, I have thought about it a lot of times in the past, and it seems like we will have very boring lives when we become adults.

Machines do most of the work, like cleaning, transportation, and even surgery, and we can't even choose our future. We were all just assigned to our groups on our last day back as Tertiary students based on probabilities and an established test programmed by the head of education. In my opinion, it is completely unfair to let machines determine what we end up becoming in society.

I stretch out my arms and yawn as most of my classmates stream out of the classroom and head to the cafeteria at the end of the hallway.

'Lunch at the hill.' Nihal nudges me as soon as I put my head on the table.

I yawn again. 'But I'm so sleepy.'

'Learning about a language does that to you,' he adds, 'but you'll need more energy for later. More energy than before since it's going to be practical.'

I hate practical classes. The act of having to sort and pack one food container after another simply bores my mind. I prefer to be doing something more hands-on that requires some skills. But I am simply out of luck.

'Honestly, can't Mrs Ruya make her lessons more interesting? I would totally pay more attention if she wouldn't just drone on and on.' Indra grumbles to no one in particular.

'We should still be grateful that we are able to learn subjects we know nothing about because there are others out there that don't have this kind of opportunity. So, you guys should stop complaining, learn a thing or two, and be grateful for the knowledge,' Faye says gently.

I know Faye is just speaking her mind, but sometimes, her words stay with me for a long time, making me second guess every move after that.

'Let's stop talking about this and go!' Nihal stands up and grabs his rucksack. He's already walking out the door when he yells out, 'Come on, guys! Keep up!'

Today, it is Faye's turn to bring lunch for us. We have made this pact to always bring our own food, since the food from the cafeteria is disgusting and pretty much inedible unless you like it mushy, bland, and tasteless.

We walk to the other end of the hallway, where an emergency exit is situated, and climb up the flight of stairs that lead us to the back exit. I'm sure there aren't a lot of other students who are even aware of this exit. We just accidentally stumbled upon it, and it has been an advantage for us ever since.

We step out of the building and are now back in civilization, out of the artificial lights inside and exposed to the bright sun.

Behind the Academy is the hill where we regularly hang out during lunchtime. We are prohibited from leaving the premises till our compulsory six hours are up, but we consider ourselves rebels. On top of that, eating in the canteen can get really stuffy, with approximately two hundred human beings—everyone forced to hear all those other voices while talking themselves.

The hike up the hill only takes a few minutes. It's not even tiring—we reach our regular hangout spot without breathing hard. We hike up here almost every day, so it has become a normal part of our daily routines.

We sit down in a circle on slightly damp grass—no one is bothered by it. Faye starts taking the containers out of her tote bag and opens them, 'Today's lunch menu is fried rice with a sprinkle of basil.'

'This looks really delicious!' Nihal announces and sniffs the food from the container. 'Thank you to Mr Li for our lunch today. I shall eat with prosper!'

Faye doesn't react to Nihal's antics, she has pretty much become accustomed to them.

We are all contentedly eating our lunch in silence when I break it off to ask Indra, 'Anything interesting happening back in your domicile that I should be aware of?' I copy his words from before just to tease him.

He gives me an annoyed look but smiles as he says, 'Just a normal day, just like how it is every day. Thank you for asking.' While playing around with his food and looking at Nihal and me, he adds, 'But I did see something interesting yesterday. I arrived on my street, and I saw Agung walking Lin home.'

'Really? Now that is something.' Nihal perks up, always wanting to know who's dating who.

Indra adds nonchalantly, 'And you know that Lin sits right beside me in class. I overheard her talking to her friends this morning that Agung confessed to her.'

Nihal gasps. 'How do you get this kind of information anyway? I would never have thought of you as such a gossip.'

'I heard some people don't take Indra seriously, so they always just slip up and reveal such information in front of him,' I answer on behalf of Indra.

'If you say so,' Indra says looking bored, already hoping for this conversation to end.

'Can we talk about something else, please?' Faye states irritatingly.

*Gladly*, I thought.

I stare up into the vast sky and utter my thoughts aloud, 'What do you guys think is out there? I mean, beyond the Central Island and even beyond the boundary.'

'No one knows and no one has survived to tell the tale,' Faye replies. 'Besides, no one, except army officers, is even allowed to leave the island. Moreover, crossing the boundary? That is just madness.'

Killen was not always a divided island. But after the war ravaged the world, our island state was split into four small islands. The war broke out before I was even born and caused massive destruction. Some countries didn't survive it. We were lucky to be a bit far from the action of what used to be the most influential countries in the world.

We are in the heart of the four islands—the Central Island. This is where the citizens live, attend the Academy, work, and where I'll definitely spend the rest of my life.

'I heard a theory that it is full of unknown demons,' Nihal states animatedly. 'Or even worse, zombies and monsters?'

'You just believe the nonsense everyone spouts,' Faye says, shaking her head.

'Do I? You also don't know what's out there, so you don't know what to believe in either,' Nihal defends himself. Then, as though to prove a point, he adds, 'I would go see what is out there and return unscathed just to prove you wrong, Faye. You mark my words.'

'Right! I bet you wouldn't even pass the Central Island before getting captured by army officers,' Faye scoffs.

Nihal stands up, 'How dare you?'

'How dare I? It's true! There isn't a single drop of blood in you that is courageous.' Faye is starting to raise her voice.

Indra and I look at each other, and we share the same thought, *Here we go again.* We focus on eating, trying to tune out their argument.

'You have no idea who you're talking to,' Nihal retorts.

'A foolish man, that is what you are,' Faye gives it back.

'And you are just a girl who can't process the idea that there are a lot of people who are greater and braver than you will ever be. Myself included.'

'Please, stop blinding yourself with lies.'

'Yeah? You want to talk about lies?'

'Nihal, don't—' I try to warn him.

'Don't you dare go there, Nihal!' Faye raises her voice.

'You just have to accept the fact that your own mother, who carried you for nine months, abandoned you with your good-for-nothing father. Clearly, you were such a burden for her that she had to run away to who knows where, leaving you all alone with your neglectful father in that house. She's probably still out there, living her life,' Nihal rants.

'Is that what you really think of me, Nihal?' Faye squawks indignantly. It doesn't take a genius to know she feels betrayed, having to hear something so harsh from someone she calls a friend. 'Then we were never friends.'

She says this in a calm voice, but I know, we all know, that she is trying to hold in her pent-up emotions. Right now, I don't know who to react to first—Nihal, for making such a crude comment when he should have known better than to broach such a sensitive subject, or Faye, comforting and remaining by her side to let her know that she is never alone.

'Wait, Faye—'

She ignores Nihal, who looks guilty, and walks away, feeling isolated.

'You've really gone overboard, Nihal! What the hell were you thinking?' I scream.

'I just—' he stammers.

'What? We're trying to comfort her, make her feel better? What were you trying to prove? Because for all I know, we're all friends here. God, you're such a jerk,' I assert.

We are silent for some time before I say, 'Indra, help me out here and talk some sense into your friend. I'll go check on Faye.'

I leave in search of my friend. I find her not too far away, looking out into the distance, her hair billowing in the wind. As my shoes crunch against the leaves on the ground, she swiftly turns around but calms down when she sees it's me.

She tries to wipe her tears with her sleeve, and I pat her shoulder in solidarity. I say in a gentle voice, 'Some friend Nihal is, huh?'

'Yeah, I'm fine. Don't worry, I'm not weak and dumb enough to take Nihal's words seriously. I know he's just a jerk and speaks without thinking sometimes.'

'Yeah, but that still doesn't make it okay.'

'I know,' she smiles at me reassuringly. 'I'm going to make him pay one day, and he's going to be sorry,' she says light-heartedly.

'That's my girl.'

'You should go. I want to be alone for a while.'

I nod, 'Okay, we'll wait for you.'

I walk away slowly and turn around to stare at her forlorn back. I just need to give her time and space, and soon enough, she will be fine.

But for now, someone needs to pay.

I return back to where the boys are sitting, and they appear to be ignoring each other. I ambush Nihal as I think back to the consequences of his words for Faye and the evident pain in her eyes.

'Seriously, Nihal. What *were* you thinking?' I say.

'I know I crossed the line. I said that without thinking, and I didn't realize what I was saying until it was too late,' Nihal says regretfully. I can see that he truly meant everything that he just said.

'Well, you'd better go and apologize.'

'Yeah.' He stands up and walks in the direction where Faye is.

*Fun lunch*, I think and continue eating. *I may seem like I'm heartless right now, but I wouldn't want perfectly fine food to go to waste, would I? That'd be a shame.*

Indra scoots closer beside me.

'Is she okay?' Indra asks worriedly.

'You know how she is—acting like she's fine when she clearly isn't. I'm really worried about her, Indra.'

'Me too.'

I look at my watch. 'We should probably get going.'

He nods his head in agreement, 'Yeah, we really should.'

'I'll call them.' I volunteer to go but don't have to go too far because the two of them are already making their way back. Nihal's eyes are downcast, no doubt still feeling guilty.

'We should go now,' Indra states when we get back to our spot.

We all collect our own trash and make a beeline down the hill. The mood has changed drastically, going from carefree to sullen. I never like when we end up arguing, especially the space in between forgiveness and acceptance. Indra remains indifferent, as always, whereas Nihal still keeps looking back and forth between the road ahead and Faye. She ignores him, treating him like a fly on the wall.

We go through the back entrance into the Academy like nothing happened. Each of us gets back to our own assigned work. Faye heads to Room 4, a training ground for the infirmary, where she is actually doing what I call good work, learning how to attend to patients. The rest of us—Nihal, Indra, and I—head to Room 5 and continue the boring job of packing food.

I remember our last day as Secondary students, when I got my results.

* * *

I have been called to the room where each one of us will find out where we will be assigned individually. Standing next to me, Faye smiles, and I confidently yet shakily enter the room. It will determine my future—my life—and I have every right to be nervous. I join one of the queues in the room, only to be greeted by a scowling instructor.

'Ahmad, is it?' He smirks, without making eye contact. He continues looking at the papers in his hands.

'Good morning, sir. My name is Puteri Aeni. Ahmad was my father's name.'

Instructors and teachers usually refer to students by their name, but for some reason, he insists on calling me by my last name.

'Your results have shown that you are most compatible to be working as a factory worker in the food industry. Well, does that not sound like fun?

You can take the papers there on the table. If you have no questions to ask, you are dismissed.'

I hesitate, feeling small for wanting to question the instructor. 'I do have a question actually now that you've reminded me. Why have I been placed in this field? Can't you, for once, listen to what we have to say, since it involves our lives, after all.'

'Excuse me?' he looks at me in disbelief, finally making eye contact with me for the first time. He seems so offended by my question, as though I have just addressed him by his name or something more horrid than. 'Are you questioning my authority? What right do you have to even speak to me?'

I repeat my question but in a higher pitch, 'I just wanted to know why I was placed in Group E? That is all.'

'Don't think so highly of yourself, Ahmad. Do you really think you belong to any other groups?' He stands up and steps closer to me. I can feel his breath on my face as he says, 'The machine has done its job, and I'm only here to deliver the information. Maybe it's because, at the end of the day, that is where you deservedly belong.'

He eyes me from head to toe and spits, 'You disgust me. Now move along. Your training session is starting soon.'

His scrutiny makes me want to cower and hide inside my domicile for good. I feel like scrubbing my body clean to make me forget ever having such unwanted attention.

'Thank you, sir,' I mumble as I snatch the papers from the table and walk out of the room before slamming the door behind me.

* * *

Now, here we are, forced to be pleased and content with having a future that we didn't have any say in whatsoever. Democracy be damned.

Both Indra and Nihal don't stop walking until they have reached their own seats far away from each other. I turn to look at Indra who gives me a worried look. With a shake of my head, I assure him that I'm fine.

I step into the room and choose a seat at the back, where I don't have to worry about the two fighters at the front who are clearly still in the mood to bicker with each other. If and when that happens, I will be way at the back and get away from all the drama and fiasco of their fights.

'Good evening, children!' comes the booming voice of Mr Nel, who is our co-teacher for our practical classes. I really like him, he's easy-going, fun, and has a great sense of humour, unlike our other co-teacher, who thinks the worst of everyone and thinks very highly of himself.

I'm glad it's Mr Nel conducting our practical class today because if it was the other teacher, it would have made my day a whole lot worse, with more drama and anger around the workroom.

'Today, we will perfect boxing food for delivery according to Killen's standards.'

Like any other day, my mind wanders, and I do what we have been assigned without much precision and thinking. I go with it, just getting it done because I can't even be bothered to care.

The shrill bell indicates the end of the day at the Academy, and I am startled back to reality.

'Hey, let's go!' Indra says, looking relieved to find me at the back.

I look up from my work, packaging the last box for today. 'Yeah, wait up. I'll be right there.'

Besides me, I hear voices going back and forth.

'What do you think the shot was for? I mean, I don't want to question the authorities, but I just find it weird. Don't you think it is?'

'As much as I want to talk about this, I have a date with my soon-to-be wife.'

I look up to see whose voices they are. It is Agung and his friend, whose name I can't recall. They walk out, and it leaves me questioning what their conversation was all about.

'Are you going to stay here overnight or what?' comes Indra's voice again as he waves his hand in front of my face. 'I don't think that's even legal.'

'Yeah, I'm coming!' I respond.

And I mean it this time. I grab my rucksack and follow Indra out of the workroom, then the Academy, to finally head home after a long day.

# Chapter 3

The front door of my domicile unlocks with a click, and I cross the threshold.

*The place is quiet. Ma must still be at the infirmary.*

I glance at the clock in the living room. It's 6.15 p.m., which means I am only five minutes later than my usual time coming back home from the Academy. I was partially held up by the crowd of people already preparing for the annual celebration of the independence of Killen.

People are already putting up posters and artworks to replace last year's remnants on the wall. Lanterns are streaming down strings that elevate the look of the city and children are already waving and running around with Killen's flag to show how proud they are of our city.

I drop my rucksack on the sofa and head straight into the bathroom. I am in dire need of a hot shower. After standing under the steaming water for almost half an hour, I grab a new set of clothes and put them on. Everyone in Killen wears the same clothes every day. A simple grey blouse with black pants.

I am about to head to my bedroom and lie down lazily on my bed for a bit when I hear a noise coming from the kitchen.

*That must be Ma.*

I head towards the kitchen and unsurprisingly, she is on her tiptoes, trying to retrieve a vase from the top of the shelf.

'Let me get that,' I say.

'You're back,' Ma says with a warm smile, even though I can clearly tell how tired she is. I push her aside, pick up a stool, place it by the counter, and reach it easily. I hand it over to her.

'Yeah. What do you need that vase for anyway?' I ask. 'I mean, it's not like we grow flowers here.'

Any kind of plants are scarce now. Only those with access and working in horticulture are lucky enough to see actual flowers bloom. I wonder what it feels like to touch and smell them.

'Your mind wandered far there,' Ma says, amused, wiping the vase with a napkin. 'What were you thinking about?'

I stare at her and snap myself out of it before she gets even more suspicious. 'Oh, just this and that.'

'You are so much like your father sometimes.'

She has a faraway look in her eyes.

*I know that look.*

'Ma,' I start, but I don't know how to continue the question, so I just drop it altogether. It wouldn't do us any good to discuss that. She always keeps to herself whenever I try to bring it up anyway.

She shrugs the look off and beams at me, 'So, what do you want for dinner?'

'Anything is fine, honestly.'

Right then, a monotonous voice is heard from the speaker, 'Citizens of Killen, please present yourself and the rest of your families to the City Hall for the quarterly assembly with the Seri Paduka Baginda, Mahsuri, Permaisuri of Killen. Those who fail to do as told will be punished under the High Law of Killen. Thank you.'

I groan, 'Is this really necessary?'

Ma chuckles, 'I know. We could have just rested at home. Alas, we must be good citizens.'

'Can we be bad just for today?' I wiggle my eyebrows.

'As much as I find that tempting, we still need to go.' Ma tuts.

The Permaisuri usually just drones on and on about the same thing all the time. Sometimes, the Permaisuri speaks, other times some high-ranking officer does. But at the end of the day, the messages are more or less the same. If there is a test to make the citizens repeat the words, everyone will succeed with flying colours.

'Come on! You heard the woman. Let's go and meet the Permaisuri.'

* * *

We take the tram to the City Hall, which is located in the heart of Killen, near the Academy. The tram is packed with citizens who are also heading to the same place.

Once there, we stand among others, their hushed tones reverberating around the place as everyone waits for the arrival of the Permaisuri.

The City Hall is an open space where everyone assembles either during the quarterly assembly of the Permaisuri, a festival, or the annual graduation at the Academy.

*Who knows what will happen to anyone who doesn't show up? I, for sure, will not be the one to find that out.*

'Ahmad, fancy seeing you here!' It is Indra.

'Yeah, I don't fancy seeing you here, man.' I appear all serious, having no energy to entertain his musings.

'Touché,' he says, placing his hand on his chest. That's Indra for you, people, dramatic at his best.

A younger boy with brown hair and familiar hazel eyes, reaching Indra's shoulders, approaches us.

'Hi, Aeni!' Adi smirks as he stands way too close for my liking. I have to swivel aside to maintain my comfort.

He is Indra's younger brother. In his words, he is the most annoying person in all of Killen. I know that deep down Indra still adores Adi. Indra doesn't really see and notice it, but he can be very overprotective of his brother and will not hesitate to punch the hell out of someone if they ever hurt or even touch him. Adi was sick a lot when they were younger and appears frail. In Indra's eyes, it's hard for him to let go of that image of Adi, even though he is well and healthy now.

I smile warmly at him, 'Hi, Adi.'

'Dude don't encourage him,' Indra whispers. But Adi has heard what he has said anyway and scowls at him.

Adi has had a crush on me ever since Indra and I first became friends. He once even said he adores me so much that he can actually see himself marrying me one day. Indra has always been opposed by the idea right from the very beginning. I really don't blame him. As much as I respect the extent of his imagination, I do not see myself marrying Adi, who I will always see as Indra's little, goofy, and innocent brother.

'Bye, Adi!' Indra lightly pushes his brother away, 'Go and find your friends instead of leeching on to me.'

'Please, you are so full of yourself.' Adi folds his arms across his chest, and soon, they are having a staring contest.

'Ugh! You're so disgusting that my eyes are burning and writhing on their own,' Indra says while pretending to rub his eyes and vomit.

'Don't be a douche,' Adi responds while the smile directed at me doesn't leave his face. He finally relents because of how childish his brother is being and waves before walking away.

We stand there, peacefully in silence, before Indra speaks, 'I have no idea what he even sees in you. I think that one of these days I might have to take him to the infirmary because there is a huge chance that he might be blind because I really can't, and refuse to, see what he sees in you.'

'Stop being so dramatic!'

He thinks for a while before adding, 'As a matter of fact, I might have to take him to see a psychiatrist because it's not healthy at all for a young teenage boy like him to think about marriage. If you ask me, I think there's something in the food because kids nowadays are seriously so weird.'

I nudge his elbow, 'You are the worst. He's still your brother.'

The intercom buzzes—indicating that the Permaisuri has arrived. Everyone around me has stopped talking and they all stand tall. As if they might be executed in case they don't.

Meanwhile, Indra and I continue our conversation. We're talking about how funny it will be if Mr Raye, the market's butcher, grows a full beard or even a pointy moustache.

We laugh quietly and I lock eyes with my ma, who is standing two rows in front of me. She points towards the stage in front of us and gives me a pointed look. She turns her head around and faces the stage ahead.

Indra has also seen the look on her face and has gone quiet, staring straight ahead. I stand there with my back hunched, kicking away pebbles on the ground.

*Permaisuri* is the word for 'queen', which originated from Sanskrit. Before you call me a history geek,

I should warn you that we must know about our Permaisuri and all that royalty stuff—I couldn't care less about. When the Permaisuri was only a teenager, her parents, who at the time had been the rulers of Killen, were brutally murdered. Their eyeballs were gouged out, they had cuts all over their bodies, even ones running across their bodies, and the worst thing of all was that the murderer hung them up on the entrance of the castle for all the people of Killen to see. To this day, no one knows the true murderer or murderers, since it didn't seem like a one-man job. People had a lot of theories about the incident, but the most absurd one I've heard is that the Permaisuri was the one who actually killed them. I refuse to believe that.

Back in the day, the castle where the royal family resides was built on the Central Island where we are all standing now. But for safety reasons—to protect against attacks and coups by the citizens—they knocked the glorious building down and built an entirely new one on an empty island on the west side of Killen within a year. No one except for the Permaisuri and her entourage—guards, maids, specialists, and who knows who else—can access it. She could even have a special shoe shiner for all I know. Anyone who tends to her is forbidden from telling anyone anything. A woman even went missing when she accidentally told her spouse something about the Permaisuri. That's how serious it is, apparently.

The Permaisuri finally appears at the edge of the stage, and I give my full attention to her. She gracefully sashays to the middle of the stage in all her glory—her red cape sweeping the floor almost obediently. Her face softens as she holds her stance and scrutinizes the citizens of Killen, ready to give her all too familiar speech that we hear once every three months.

The current Permaisuri has been ruling Killen for the past six years, and to this day, she looks dauntingly young, as though she has never aged after all this time. Her face is constantly taut and serious—I have never once seen her smile. Nor has anyone else, I presume. Her brunette hair is tied up in a bun at the top of her head.

She is beautiful, no one can deny that.

'Good evening, citizens of Killen.' She has a thick Killean accent, clear of any hint of raspiness.

Everyone gives their undivided attention to her, even though our ears are already bored hearing the same things spouting out of her.

'This evening, I will not remind all of you of the enforcement of the laws of Killen and what actions you, as citizens, will face if you dare to not abide by them.' She pauses. 'I am going to show you.'

Talk about getting straight to the point.

Upon hearing her last statement, everyone starts buzzing, turning around to one another, and getting more curious as time passes by. Everyone is heatedly speaking and telling one another of their own predictions.

Despite the voices coming from all around City Hall, the Permaisuri's voice can be heard even from miles away. She nods to one of the guards and says, 'Bring them in.'

Immediately, the guards drag out three boys to the centre of the stage. Pure fear about what their punishment will be is plastered all over their faces. They look younger than fourteen years old and are obviously still in the Secondary group at the Academy.

Permaisuri points her finger at them, as if them being huddled on the stage isn't clarifying who she's referring to, 'These three young men in front of you have done the one unforgivable act under our laws.'

She pauses, and the area is so quiet that you could hear a pin drop. Everyone is anticipating what she will say next.

I suddenly feel like a ball of nerves, afraid of what might come next. Never in my life have I experienced or witnessed the Permaisuri's wrath. Beside me, Indra looks tense.

'They tried to trespass out of the Central Island, heading towards Linggi Island with a raft they made on their own.'

We are all overcome with shock, and at the same time, we fear what's about to happen to the three boys. They look so young standing on the stage right beside Permaisuri with nothing to protect them. The youngest looks like he's in his first year of Secondary. I just don't think this should be happening to them. I mean, sure, what were they thinking when they broke the law? But, at the same time, they are still just a bunch of children. I mean, look at them! They look so innocent and so scared of their fates and for their lives.

Every single citizen of Killen, young and old, knows better than to cross, or even try to pass out of, the Central Island. It is the number one act that is legally prohibited. No one has ever done it or been caught to find out about the punishment.

For the first time in the history of Killen, these boys tried to cross the island. This will also be the first time we will find out what their punishment will be.

'They are clearly uncivilized and deserve punishment,' Permaisuri's voice fills the void. 'They shall live the rest of their years on Linggi Island, where they wanted to be in the first place. In a wasteland filled with darkness and nightmares.'

'NO! PLEASE!' a woman cries out, her tears evident in her voice. She is pushing everyone around her as she rushes towards the stage.

I am startled by the woman, who looks devastated. I look in the direction of Ma, but she has her eyes on the woman.

All eyes and ears go back and forth between the woman and Permaisuri—all too scared to react. The woman is sobbing hard, her round eyes are misty, with big fat tears running down her face. Her pleading yet angry face looks as red as the Permaisuri's cape.

'I'm sorry?' Permaisuri asks. She seems taken aback by this woman's act of defiance.

'Please,' she begs, her knees are nearly buckling to the ground. 'Please spare them—my children. They are the only family I have left. I don't know what I will do with my life without them in it. They are my rays of sunshine and rainbows on a rainy day.'

Her sobs are getting louder, and she is struggling to breathe.

I steal a glance towards Ma, and she gives me a pitiful look. I give her a weak smile in return even though I am dreading what might happen next. Part of me is rooting for the family averting their impending doom yet another part of me—being a law-abiding citizen of Killen—understands the clear consequences of breaking a law.

The Permaisuri snickers. 'They have broken the high law. Now, they will face the consequences.'

'Please, they are only children.' The woman is relentless and continues speaking after sobbing for a while, 'What kind of a human being are you? How could you even bear to think up the idea of killing children?'

Everyone is silent. Any sensible person here knows not to go against the Permaisuri's words. But then no parent will be in a sensible state of mind if their children are facing any danger.

'Break the law and go against my words, and you will pay for it. What is the point of having a law and then pleading for me to make exceptions to it?' she scoffs. 'Now, I don't have time for this.'

'Take the mother and her children to the deserted island and leave them to the beast,' Permaisuri commands the guards without letting her gaze stray from the woman.

My heart stops, the nerves are getting the better of me.

The mother and her children yell in protest as they are dragged away.

No one dares to contradict the Permaisuri's order or even dares to move or so much as much as blink. She looks at the crowd one last time, as if seeing right through our weak souls with her presence. 'Take this as a warning and a lesson.'

She doesn't wait a second longer, walking away, leaving City Hall.

# Chapter 4

Ma nudges me, gives me a reassuring smile, and tells me that I wasn't the only one who just witnessed the unfortunate event at the City Hall. She wraps her arm around my waist and says, 'Let's go back home.'

We bid goodbye to Indra who leaves in search for his own family. We walk the entire way back home in silence. Both of us are out of words and grieving for the mother and her children.

Everyone here has heard of what's in their fate and what kind of beast conquers that deserted island. No one has said it out loud, but it seems plausible that that could have been the last time anyone ever saw that family.

Even in the tram, most of the adults have been stunned into silence, but the children continue talking animatedly while trying to grab their parents' attention. Everyone must be experiencing a roller coaster of emotions. Especially those who have children of their own and who love them with everything they can and more. A bonded family, specifically a parent, will, no doubt, feel the impact of this event.

We enter our domicile and both of us are just standing there at the entrance—partially embracing the comfortable silence that surrounds us.

'You know, I used to work with the lady at the infirmary. Her name is Maya and she has had it really rough ever since her husband passed away. I can't imagine how hard this must be for her,' Ma says.

I reach for her hand and say, 'That sucks.' I didn't know what else to say. I'm not the best at comforting people.

'Are you hungry?' Ma asks.

'Yeah,' I reply because my stomach has started to grumble, demanding to be fed since over an hour ago. What can I say? I am still a growing teenager after all.

She heads to the kitchen, 'I'll cook something for you, but I don't have the energy to eat tonight. So, you'll have to eat alone.'

'That's fine, Ma. You know what, as a matter of fact, I think I'll just go out and find something to eat,' I suggest. 'I'll head over to Pak Mat's place and see if Indra is up to join me.'

She nods and gives me a small smile. 'Do you need any money?'

'I'll use my allowance. Don't worry about it,' I assure her.

She looks dazed and far away from our conversation. She must not be in the mood for anything after what we all just witnessed. I place my hands on her shoulders in an attempt to console her. 'Ma, are you okay? Do you need me to stay with you? I can just heat up my dinner if you need the company.'

She waves me off. 'I'm fine. You go and fill up your massive appetite, okay?'

I give her a suspicious look. 'Are you sure?'

'Yes, I'm very sure. Now you go ahead before your stomach starts grumbling again.'

I nod and add a joke of my own to cheer her up a bit, 'After all, I'm sure that there are still some food vendors who want extra money in their pockets, right?'

She only responds with a small, half-hearted smile, 'I'll be in my room. I won't wait up. Go have fun while you're young.'

She caresses my right cheek, walks away and closes her bedroom door behind her.

* * *

Unlike Faye and Nihal's domiciles, Indra's was just a short walk away from mine. On my way there, my mind keeps replaying the Permaisuri's words and the expressions of the family. I worry about Ma, who must be shaken up even though she tries to act like it hasn't bothered her.

I am so in my head that I missed Indra's domicile. So, I have to snap out of it and retrace my steps.

Once I get there, I ring the doorbell, and a second later, Adi opens the door. When he sees that it's me standing on their front doorstep, he gives me a toothy grin, but it doesn't quite reach his eyes like it usually does. The event has really taken a toll on everyone, even the playful and vibrant Adi.

'Oh, hi, Aeni!' he says.

I smile, out of politeness, and say, 'Hey, Adi. Is Indra here?'

'Yeah, he's inside.' Adi's staring at the ground like it is the most interesting thing he has ever seen.

'Can you call him for me?' I ask while trying to catch his attention.

'Sure,' he says, his gaze never leaving the ground.

'Adi, *sayang*, who's at the door?' Adi's and Indra's mother asks as she walks to the front door and sees me standing awkwardly on her doorstep. She looks at her son, who is standing there like a statue. She shakes her head seeing her son like that, caught up in his own thoughts. 'I'm assuming you're here for Indra?'

I smile at her for finally getting me out of this uncomfortable situation. She takes the smile I can barely muster as an answer and tells me to wait here as she goes back inside to call for Indra. A moment later, he appears, hair tousled and shirt wrinkled. The usually pristine-looking Indra now looks shaken. Seeing Adi by the door, he suddenly looks mischievous.

'Adi!' Indra yells in his ear, and Adi stumbles back in surprise.

'You scared me!' Adi punches his chest in retort.

Indra laughs at his brother's response. 'You need to chill, little brother.'

Adi glares at Indra. 'And you need to stop being a twit, brother.'

Adi storms off, and Indra yells out, 'Love you, too!'

I smile at their antics, and somewhere deep inside me, I feel a tinge of jealousy at their sibling bond. *How would my life have turned out if I had a younger sibling? Would I take pleasure in making fun of them or would I play the role of an elder sibling, just as I sometimes imagine I would if I had one?* I push the thought away to the back of my mind and say to Indra, 'I'm heading out to eat at our usual place, do you want to join me?'

'Sure. I'll go tell my mom first before she jumps to conclusion and gets super pissed.' He walks back inside to inform his mother.

He returns a moment later and gives me thumbs up, indicating that his mother has allowed them to go.

We walk the short distance to our favourite *mamak* place, Pak Mat's. We head inside and sit down in our usual booth beside the display window. We have been coming here ever since we are allowed to go around by ourselves. They serve all kinds of our local delicacies like *nasi lemak*, cheese *naan*, *kari ikan*, dim sum, *cendol*, and so much more. Just name whatever you want, Pak Mat's will surely have it. It's what makes the mamak so special.

The waitress takes our orders—we don't even need to see the menu because we have learned and know it all by heart. The waitress leaves us with our rumbling thoughts to take other customers' orders.

'Wow, fancy seeing you here,' I hear someone say, standing next to our table.

It's Faye. Nihal is standing beside her and is pleased to see the two of us. They appeared together, so they must have called a truce, or they're just ignoring the elephant in the room. Still, it's nice to see that they've worked it out.

'What a coincidence. Ma didn't feel like cooking, so I invited Indra along. What about you two? How did you end up together?' I say looking back and forth between them.

Faye shrugs, 'My *baba* is not home so I decided to look for my own dinner.'

Nihal adds, 'I didn't like the vibes in my house, it's so gloomy and my *amma* keeps talking about what happened at the City Hall. I just needed some air and met Faye on the way. She didn't invite me here, but I tagged along anyway.'

I pat the space beside me and gesture to them. 'Come, sit down. The more the merrier.'

Faye settles down beside me while Indra and Nihal sit across.

'But that was really something else, wasn't it? I know I'm not the only one with chills running down my spine. It was so scary, I tell you. My legs were literally trembling, and I had to hold on to a poor, old lady for support, and she looked at me like, *really?* You know, since it should be the other way around,' Faye says.

'About what happened at the City Hall?' I ask for confirmation, and she rolls her eyes at me, giving me a look that says, *obviously*.

'What do you guys think the beast is?' Nihal asks, finally stepping into the conversation and shivering at the mere thought. 'Or whatever it is out there, waiting for them the moment they step foot on the island?'

'Who knows what it is? But I'm not going to be the one to find out,' Faye says in a matter-of-fact voice.

'No one is asking you to.' Indra states the obvious.

'Geez, you guys. I was just saying it as a joke. Not literally.' Nihal defends himself. 'But I know it's not something to joke about. It's just wrong on every level. I mean, sure, a beast sounds cool if we're talking about those old books and movies. But knowing that they exist, real and within reach, is just crazy to me.'

The table is silent, and this time, no one bothers to continue the conversation further. Usually, we are churning with excitement as the smell of the food wafts up to us, anticipating the pleasure it will bring to our stomachs. But now, we are so deep in our own thoughts that no one even looks up when the waiter places the food on the table.

It is as though, suddenly, we have become people with no reactions whatsoever. Like robots who only act without thinking first.

We all eat our food silently, until Nihal accidentally drops his fork on the porcelain plate a little too loudly. It catches the attention of other customers in the mamak, including us. We all look up at him, and he has a faraway look on his face. I am slightly annoyed at the sudden, noisy intrusion. Even though I can't seem to remember exactly what I was thinking about.

'This is getting too uncomfortable.' Faye sighs. 'If all of you are going to act and be this way, I might as well have just stayed back home.'

'What do you expect us to say when you haven't said much yourself,' I say bluntly. I mean, she can't just expect us to talk like nothing has happened while she herself has not responded to anything. It seems pointless to me.

'You're right. I just wish that we could continue being like we used to be.' She sighs. 'This deafening silence is killing me.'

Nihal stares at her. 'Well, a family's fate was just announced right in front of our faces. Obviously, none of us will be fine with that. Some people just take more time to process things and move on. Sorry, we're not all like you, Faye.'

If someone didn't know Faye, I have no doubt they'd think she's heartless. Who knows? Maybe she is after all. She's always the only one unfazed by any suspicious incidents or even horrifying ones, like the one we experienced not long ago.

We all continue being deep in our thoughts. No one even bothers to respond. Usually, Nihal keeps our conversation going. I guess the incident has left him dumbstruck too.

Suddenly, Faye stands up a little too quickly, making her chair screech. 'I'm heading back then.'

She places a wad of cash on the table and leaves the mamak in a hurry. Heading back home, I suppose.

'What was all that about?' Indra asks, worry etched on his face.

My brow furrows, 'She was just fine before that, right?'

Nihal shakes his head, 'I haven't a clue. I've noticed that she has been acting a little weird and distant lately. Like something is really bothering her.'

I stand up, and they both look up at me, 'I think I'm going to go and catch up with her. I'm leaving. See you tomorrow.'

I race towards her house, looking out for her shoulder-length brunette hair, but it is nowhere to be seen.

*She won't have gone too far.*

My breath is growing short as I near her domicile row. I run all the way in hopes that I'll catch up to her before she arrives.

*I guess I'm wrong then. Wow! The girl sure walks fast.*

I knock on Faye's door, and her father greets me as he opens the door.

'Hello, Mr Li,' I greet him and become the politest person in the whole of Killen, since the man is super intimidating, and I would not like to be on his bad side. I might die and I mean that literally. He is that stern and serious.

Mr Li works in the defence and military department, which means he has one of the coolest jobs and is rarely home. Our group of friends dug up some information about what he really does but he has never nor will he ever utter, even squeak, about it. Even his wife doesn't know what he really does.

*If you want discretion, Mr Li is the man for it.*

'Is Faye back yet?' I ask the man who has the same exact brown hair and hazel eyes as his daughter. Faye looks so much like her father that she even reminds me of Mr Li's silent demeanour sometimes.

He stares at me confusedly. 'No. She told me that she's out with Nihal. Aren't the four of you always together?'

'We were together, but she suddenly left. I thought she was already home, but I guess she isn't back yet?'

'That's strange. Maybe she had to go and get something at the store?' Mr Li suggests. 'But I'm sure that she'll be back home soon.'

'Yeah.' I pause, but don't ponder too much over it. 'Anyway, I better head back home. It was nice seeing you again, Mr Li.'

'And I, you.'

I head back home, which is just a short walk from the Li's. Our domiciles are only a couple of rows apart, so we often walk to the Academy together.

I reach my domicile and unlock it. I close the door behind me and make a beeline to Ma's room. I silently open the door and am met with the sight of her cozily curled in bed, asleep. I don't bother her and immediately close the door behind me and make my way to my bedroom. I head straight to my inviting bed and fall into it, making myself comfortable and letting sleep take me away.

# Chapter 5

The clock chimes its daily morning alarm—announcing the arrival of the day to everyone and demanding to be heard even from miles away. I get it, it's time to wake up, and I am certainly not happy about it. I fell asleep at around 9.00 last night, and yet, I find that I haven't had enough sleep. Though I'm sure I've slept way past eight hours, which totally meets the requirement of beauty sleep.

*I'm sure I'm not the only one who feels that way, right?*

I wake up groggily and quickly head for the bathroom before I get late and have to rush.

I get dressed and go to the kitchen in search for food that I can munch on as I head to the Academy. I open the cupboard and shuffle some boxes of food. I find granola bars and grab a few because breakfast is the most important meal of all, and it's not good to leave one's stomach empty, as Ma says multiple times every day. Besides, I do have quite the appetite.

'Aeni, are you dressed yet for the Academy?' Ma asks from across the hallway.

'Yes!' I yell back.

She chuckles. 'I overslept, Aeni! For the first time ever! Can you believe that?'

'It feels amazing, doesn't it?' I counter so that she finally understands why I often relish the pleasure of sleeping in, especially on the weekends. I'm sure it must have been a really new experience for her.

'I'll be really quick. Wait up for me, okay? We'll head out together,' she hurriedly slams the bathroom door close.

I glance at the big clock in the corner of the living room—9.35 a.m. Anyway, Ma and I always walk to the tram station together—when I'm not already running late, that is. And today, I have just enough time to spare and linger around.

I still have time. And I will get there in time. Not to worry. Just watch as I embark on a personal journey to be punctual.

I sit down, open up a packet of granola bar, and eat it slowly—tasting every flavour, savouring it. Immediately, I open up another packet and bite right into it. These things are actually good when you're on the go. I don't know why I haven't noticed this before.

Before I know it, both of the granola bars have been emptied out in my once-empty stomach. I glance at the clock again—9.45 a.m.

We really should get going now. Ma should have been ready. What's taking her so long?

'Ma?' I call out. Well, this is weird. She has never been late in her life. I have not inherited my punctuality from her, so this is odd. I'm certain that I heard the sound of doors opening and closing just a moment ago.

Yet, no answer. Only silence.

'Ma?' I call again, louder this time.

Did she doze off? A bathroom related activity that she can't get out of and avoid? Is it nature calling? But if that was the case, I'm sure she would have replied to me when I called out for her.

I walk towards her bedroom, 'Ma?'

I find her in her bedroom, standing in the middle of the room, staring in the distance unblinkingly. I have never in my life seen her this way before. Has she lost it? What is happening? Why is she frozen solid like she is no longer living?

I panic and remain undecided on what to do about this sudden turn of events. I feel like asking someone for help, but there's clearly no one around.

I check for her pulse and put a hand under her nose. She is still breathing and very much alive. I heave a sigh of relief.

'Ma?' I ask slowly, placing my hand on her shoulder, trying to get her out of her trance.

Her head turns around but the voice that comes out of her mouth isn't hers, 'Subject 365 is locked in.'

What was that?

I shake Ma back and forth, trying to get her to wake up and return to me. She turns her head to look at me and a nasal voice comes out of her mouth again, 'Subject breached in area 55.'

What is happening to her? Is she possessed or something? Did she eat something bad? Poison?

Tears start brimming in my eyes. I stare at Ma, really stare at her. The wrinkles that line her face, her stout nose, and those hazel eyes that she constantly brags about—my dad would always talk so lovingly about how beautiful they are and how they can move mountains.

One by one, my tears start to fall.

She finally blinks. 'Aeni?' she asks in her all-too-familiar voice that never fails to make me feel warm.

I quickly brush away my tears with the back of my hand and say, 'Ma?'

Relief overcomes me and my knees feel like buckling in defeat. There were so many scenarios going through my head, yet I feel like the past few minutes never happened. Could it all just have been a lucid dream?

'Aeni? What are you still doing here? Aren't you going to be late to the Academy? You're going to be late now,' Ma admonishes, hands on her waist in clear disapproval as though the past few minutes never happened.

I hug her tight, so afraid of losing her. In that moment, I don't care that I am running late. Detention and a lot of nagging and scolding can line up and wait for me for all I care because I never want what just transpired to happen again.

'Ma, I love you. Don't lose yourself. I'm right here if you need me.' I look at her one more time and hurry away. I don't want her to see me crumble.

I glance at the clock—9.53 a.m.

That's strange. It feels like an eternity has passed while it has just been a couple of minutes.

Maybe I'm the one who is losing my mind.

I grab my rucksack, which I left on the kitchen floor, and rush to the Academy.

I guess I've a lot of things to ponder today.

* * *

'Hey, Aeni! Wait up!' Faye says while sprinting over to me in the corridor outside our classroom. A lot of students are still milling around outside, taking their time to go inside their respective classes, and it's already 10.15 a.m. Classes should have begun by now.

'Oh, hey!' I greet her.

'You were going so fast there,' Faye says.

'Was I? I didn't realize,' I admit.

'You didn't realize a lot of things. Like you almost ran into a junior.'

I stare at her, not really absorbing a thing she's saying.

'Earth to Aeni!' Faye is waving her arms in front of me.

'What?' I give her a weird and annoyed look. I sigh. 'I really don't have time for this. We should be in our class right now. What is everyone still doing out here in the corridor?'

'Classes will begin at 10.30 this morning. Didn't you hear the announcement?' Faye frowns. 'What's going on? Is something bothering you?'

'It's nothing. I just have a lot of things in my mind right now, that's all,' I clarify.

'If you say so.'

I remember about last night's events and the question is already out there before I realize it. 'Where did you go after you left the mamak yesterday?'

'What do you mean?' Faye asks, trying not to look me in the eye.

'I followed you—'

'What do you mean you followed me?' She cuts me off, eyes wide.

'I tried to catch up with you when you left the mamak but it was as though you vanished into thin air. So, where did you go?'

She lets out a breath, as though a secret that she's been hiding was about to be exposed, but it was a false alarm.

*What is she hiding?*

'You can tell me anything, you know. I won't tell anyone if you don't want me to. Not even Indra.' I look at her straight in the eye.

She fakes a laugh. 'What are you talking about? I have nothing to hide. Absolutely nothing. Why are you jumping to conclusions?'

'Okay.' I say. 'But where did you go last night? I even went over to your house.'

'I just had to . . . uh . . . buy . . . uhhh . . . you know . . . st . . . stuff. Girl stuff.' She stutters, looking around, making sure no one is listening, but it still doesn't convince me.

Faye only stutters when she's nervous. Why would she even be nervous around me? We have been friends for more than ten years.

'Faye, come on! Tell me the truth.' I try to get the truth out of her. I don't know why I'm so persistent this morning—it is so unlike me. If she's hiding something from me, from the rest of us, then she has every right to.

Then, why am I acting this way?

'I am!' her voice is a pitch higher than usual and some of the students turn their heads towards her. This is yet another symptom of her being nervous. We once teased her for having the most typical signs of nervousness. That's what friends do, right? We tease each other.

Or am I just getting suspicious for no particular reason because of what happened at home? Or am I just overreacting about the whole thing, and it is all just happening in my mind? Ugh, now I'm getting a headache from overthinking.

For the second time, I ask myself: *Am I losing myself?*

'Faye?' I ask, hopefully for the last time.

She looks at me, and it's a look that I have never seen before. She's looking at me as though I am her number one enemy, not her friend.

'I'm trying to be your friend here. You can tell me.' I give her an encouraging look. I know I should just drop it, but something in the back of my mind is niggling at me to find out what she's hiding. Yet, another part of me tells me that you should never push a girl to her limit.

Warning: Bad idea! Abort mission!

Faye starts speaking, 'Well—'

'Hey, guys!' Nihal is walking towards us. If he wasn't my friend, I would've told him to scram right about now.

Faye looks about the interruption caused by our friend, who is bouncing towards us. He appears to be his usual self as though the dispute between him and Faye didn't happen just yesterday.

'Hey!' Nihal is breathless when he finally reaches us.

Indra follows suit, 'Hey.'

He gives me a knowing look as though he's able to read the room. I nod my head in greeting.

'What were you guys talking about? It seems to have been heated.' He asks looking unbothered. He's either really dense or absolutely oblivious.

I say, 'It's about yesterday.'

Simultaneously, Faye says, 'Nothing!'

We look at each other and she quickly averts her eyes from me.

'We should probably head inside the class now. It's almost 10.30,' Indra announces. We are a bit surprised that this has come from him because he's usually the one who stalls the most when heading into class.

We all agree and walk the short distance into our classroom. Indra grabs my arm and silently tells me to tell him about what happened later. I agree as everyone settles down in their assigned seats and waits for the arrival of our history teacher, Mr Khan.

# Chapter 6

'Who can share with the class why Killen is a monarchy?' Mr Khan asks, and he looks hopeful that someone is actually going to answer his question even when their answer may be wrong. Mr Khan always accepts everyone's answers seriously, regardless of whether they are true or false. That's the reason he is so loved by his students.

A student in the back raises his hand. When Mr Khan nods at him, he asks, 'What does a monarchy mean?'

Any other teacher would dismiss or get annoyed at him for not knowing what the term means but Mr Khan pushes his glasses on the bridge of his nose and smiles warmly, 'Good question, Mikail. The term and the true meaning of monarchy is a system of government in a city wherein one person reigns, usually a king or queen. The authority, or crown, in a monarchy is generally inherited. The ruler, or monarch, is often only the head of state, not the head of government. And for our governed city of Killen, the one who reigns is none other than our Seri Paduka Baginda, Mahsuri, Permaisuri of Killen.'

'Is everyone clear about the meaning of a city ruled by a monarch?' Everyone murmurs with yeses and Mr Khan continues today's lesson.

'Before we continue, I would still like to hear your answers regarding my first question. The question of why our prosperous city of Killen is reigned by a monarchy? Who would like to give it a try?'

Mr Khan raises his right arm in the air to encourage the students to attempt answering. A student in the front row answers in a sure and confident voice, 'The reason is there is a balance in the power and continued progress as stated in our laws.'

Mr Khan ponders what he just said, 'A very good try, but I'm afraid your answer doesn't quite answer the whole question and was not accurate enough. Still, I like your answer and that was a very good try. Thank you for having an opinion and sharing it with the whole class.'

Mr Khan looks at the rest of the students and asks, 'Would anyone else like to attempt the question?'

He walks to his desk, pushes a few buttons on his tablet, and a few seconds later, the screen is projected on its bigger counterpart for the whole class to see. 'Here is a chart describing how Killen gradually transformed into a monarchy. It is impossible to discuss this matter without going back to the very foundation of our city—how it was built and how it remains peaceful to this day. So, in order to fully grasp the idea of why Killen is a monarchy, we shall travel back through history to a time when war had ravaged the world. We will find our answers as we go through the next few classes.'

I have pretty much zoned out what he's saying and explaining in front of the class. I hear what he's saying clearly, but it never travels to my brain, where I can process it. My mind wanders to this morning, to yesterday, anywhere and everywhere my mind can go.

The next hour is filled with half sentences that make no sense to me.

'. . . nuclear bombs . . .'

'Aircrafts were falling from the skies . . .'

'The war caused major damage . . .'

'. . . countries big or small turned to almost nothing . . .'

'. . . never existed . . .'

'Our founder has . . .'

'After years . . . missiles and any major weapon never stop firing.'

'A man who I have met and heard stories from described it as the end of the world, absolutely chaotic and apocalyptic.'

Mr Khan claps his hands, and I sit up straighter, stepping out of my daydream.

'We shall continue the discussion next week. Thank you, class. You are all dismissed.'

He's not even the kind of teacher who reprimands and calls us out for not focusing or sleeping during his classes. He smiles at us, bidding us goodbye as we stream out of the classroom. I feel guilty about it.

I really do, and I'll try better next time. You have my word, Mr Khan.

'That was a very interesting topic we just learned. I am in awe! It was just . . . how do I explain and describe it? It was basically just wow!' Nihal exclaims.

'It was okay.' Indra shrugs, clearly not enthusiastic at all about learning.

'I've known about it for some time now. You would have known about it earlier too if you'd have read a book or two from the library,' Faye states while placing her books inside her rucksack.

'You don't have to be so cocky. Not everyone spends their precious free time acquiring knowledge like you do.' Nihal rolls his eyes. He turns to Indra and mutters, 'What a know-it-all.'

Indra just smiles in return, and he looks at me like, here we go again. I try to stop them, 'Enough. Aren't you guys tired of arguing? I, for one am very tired of having to listen to both of you bicker all the time lately.'

Faye slings her rucksack on her shoulder. She simply cannot let it go, as she retorts, 'Is there something wrong about it if I do spend my precious free time that way? Is it socially unacceptable? Is that how you think it is? Come on, we live in the thirty-first century. Haven't you learned anything from the past?'

'Of course you have jumped to conclusions. Just like you always do!' Nihal exclaims, clearly dissatisfied.

Faye stares at him. 'When have I ever?'

Nihal stares back, clearly annoyed with her.

Before they get into another argument, Indra steps in as the middleman. 'That's enough, you two. We're so tired hearing both of you bicker like children. I don't want to hear it anymore. For the sake of everyone else, please stop. Right, Aeni?'

I nod my head in agreement and give him a high five in support. I raise my shoulders in an act of defiance, slump my upper body on the table and turn my head to the other side. I really don't want to be involved with their drama. Yes, they're my friends, and I do not like causing confusion and misunderstandings between them. If you ask me, I'm always choosing the middle ground from the sidelines.

'You know what? I agree with you two. I'm also tired of arguing.' Faye sighs, 'I'm off to the library if anyone needs me because the book I wanted to borrow is available. And I'm not going to let anyone snatch it up. Especially Agung.' She starts walking away and stops at the doorway. 'See you guys later.'

'That was annoying. Does she think I want to argue with her all the time too?' Nihal walks out of the classroom without a word.

Indra sighs, shaking his head as he sits back. He turns to me and says something that I don't catch. I'm looking into the distance. Indra clears his throat, and I turn to look at him and see him frowning.

'Seriously, Aeni? What has gotten into you?'

His tone is clearly concerned, I still don't reply.

He kneels down to look me in the eye. 'Hey, are you okay? What happened?'

I try to brush it aside as nothing. 'What do you mean? I'm fine.'

'Come on, Aeni. I know you. We've been friends forever, and I can clearly see something is bothering you. You can tell me, I'm all ears.'

'I don't feel like it. Maybe later?' I muster up a smile to assure him. He looks resigned as he hoists me up from the chair. 'Come on, we should head to the cafeteria to grab something to eat.'

'I'll pass. You go.'

'Okay.'

Now that the hall has settled down as everyone heads downstairs to the cafeteria, I am finally left alone with my rumbling thoughts. The whole lunch break, I remain in class. With only three minutes to spare, I go down the flight of stairs and head for practical.

* * *

It is another uneventful day at the Academy. The four of us barely talk or even see each other throughout the rest of the day. The students around me are talking loudly and being their cheerful selves as they wait for their teacher, who never arrives. I feel like my thoughts are even louder than all of their talking combined.

The clock chimes, indicating the end of the Academy for the day. I quickly make my way to the ground floor and head straight towards the tram station to finally just be with myself, alone. I think that I may have overtired myself today—putting double the force I can even handle into certain things.

I stare up at the sky as the clouds intermingle. I bask in the rays of sunlight and feel the warmth that comes with it. You never know what might happen after this. 'Take chances,' my dad would say.

'Aeni! Wait up, dude.' Indra says from across the street. When he finally catches up to me, he says, 'Where are you heading off to so quickly?'

'Home?' I say questioningly.

'So soon?'

I shrug my shoulders, 'I'm just feeling tired and would really like to lie down on my bed.'

'Sure thing.' He adds, 'What was this morning all about?'

'What about it?'

'What was the intense conversation with Faye?' Indra asks, arching one of his eyebrows.

'Nothing. It's just girl talk. It's none of your concern.'

'Are you two keeping secrets from me?'

'Really, it's nothing.'

'Is this what's got you so worked up today?'

I shake my head, 'It's nothing.'

'But you already promised you were going to tell me all about it.'

'I didn't promise anything. You were the one making assumptions.'

'Okay, then.' He finally gives up and drops the subject.

We walk in silence until we arrive at the tram station. Other familiar faces from the Academy are waiting for the tram too but there's no sight of Nihal or Faye.

'Can I ask you something?' I whisper.

'Why are you whispering?' Indra jokes, 'Do you have a crush on me?'

'Don't be ridiculous!' I feel like slapping him right then and there, but I hold myself back. Yet I can't stop my cheeks from blushing. I immediately try to forget what he just said and focus on the serious matter I'm trying to broach.

'Okay, okay! I was just kidding.'

'Did anything strange happen at your domicile this morning?' I stare at the surroundings, looking out in case there might be a chance that others could be eavesdropping on our conversation. You never know these days. Anyone could be lurking around, snooping.

'Strange?' He gives me a dubious look.

'Yeah.'

'Not that I know of.' But I've piqued his interest, so he adds, 'What exactly happened to you this morning?'

'It was Ma.'

'Was she sick?' Indra asks, actually looking worried.

'No.'

And I tell him everything. Not the part where I shed a few tears. That should only be known by me and kept in the back of my memory.

'That is strange.'

I give him a *could-you-be-more-obvious* look.

'I think I would've reacted the way you did too.'

The tram arrives, and we stand in line, just like everyone else, in a disciplined manner to get in—no pushing or shoving involved.

It doesn't take long for us to arrive at our destination—the domicile area—and I finally muster up the courage to ask him, feeling so much better after talking about this morning's incident, 'Didn't you notice that there is just something different and off about Faye?'

He thinks about it, before saying, 'A bit, yeah.'

'Yesterday, I couldn't catch up with her after she left from the mamak place so I went over to her domicile. But she wasn't there.' I pause, glancing at Indra to see if he's still listening. He is, so I continue, 'This morning, I asked her where she went and she seemed nervous. You know how she is when she's nervous, she was stuttering and all that.'

'She's definitely hiding something. Should we go and corner her or something?'

I shake my head, 'No, she's our friend. No matter how suspicious it is, we should still respect her privacy.'

We arrive at my domicile, and I unlock the door.

Indra asks me, 'Do you mind if I crash here for a few hours?'

'Don't you always?'

I enter and am shocked by the state of the interior. The tables and chairs are upside down, drawers are open, things have been thrown on the floor, and it smells like something died in here.

'What the hell?' I exclaim in alarm, a pitch higher than usual.

Indra looks around warily, assessing the area. 'I think we should take a look around. See if anything is missing. We don't often hear about burglary cases, but it's best to be extra cautious, just in case.'

I nod. 'Good idea. I'll go look around the rooms, and you stay here in the living room.'

I walk to the hallway and check out the whole place, not missing a single corner. The only parts that have been trashed are the living area, kitchen, and my bedroom. Ma's bedroom and the toilet remain untouched. Just like how I left them this morning.

I return to the living area. Indra is putting everything back where it is usually placed.

'What's the verdict?' he asks. Leave it up to him to use fancy words in a situation like this.

'Only my room and these areas have been trashed.' I look around the room, 'Its suspicious, isn't it? That they left my ma's room completely untouched.'

'That is weird.'

The doorbell rings.

'I'll get it.' Indra opens the front door.

I hear muffled voices, and Indra comes in along with Nihal and Faye. Looks like they have reconciled. I wonder who sucked it up to say they were wrong first. I'm placing my bet on Nihal.

'We thought you'd be he—' Faye starts saying before she stops to take in the mess.

'Wow! This is something to relieve your stress, isn't it?' Nihal continues to look around my trashed house. How does he always have the energy to joke around in every situation?

'It's not funny.' I give him a look indicating that this is not the time and place to joke around.

'Okay, I know. I was just saying,' he rubs his neck before saying, 'Do you need our help?'

'Sure,' I say while walking towards my bedroom. I remain on my own, and I can hear their voices picking up, but I don't bother trying to listen in on their conversation. My mind is fuddled, and I need to clear all of this before Ma comes back home.

I kneel down to pick up papers that are scattered on the floor. Whoever did this, and if I ever find the person who was behind this, will be very, very sorry.

Someone enters the room, and I don't bother looking up. I just want to get the place clean and catch up on some sleep. I'm just so awfully tired, and this situation is definitely not helping at all.

'Here, let me help you,' Faye says while picking up other things that have been thrown around by the person behind this mess.

We pick everything up and place it on the table, which is also not where it rightfully belongs—in the corner of my room, not upside down on the floor—before we put it back.

'Aeni, look, about this morning, I—'

'Forget about it. Just forget I ever said anything,' I cut her off.

'No. It's just,' she pauses, 'I just wasn't ready to tell you, any of you guys, yet.'

'Okay, we get it. We're not that important to you,' I snap, irritation getting the best of me.

Faye looks hurt by my words. 'What are you talking about? Of course, you all are.'

'Sure,' I add in a mocking tone.

'What is the matter with you? This is about me, what I have to deal with, it doesn't concern you, and it doesn't eat you up slowly day by day as each day passes by,' Faye raises her voice.

I don't want to see the painful look on her face, so I keep my gazed fixed on the floor. Wanting to end this conversation, I relent, 'Fine.'

'Look who's being the jackass now, huh? Just when I have finally found the courage to talk about it, you act this way, don't you?' She looks at me, but I don't bother looking back. I continue busying myself with cleaning up my room. I'm just so tired of everything.

She storms out of the room, and I hear the front door slam shut.

*Great.*

# Chapter 7

The next day, I head over to the Academy as if it is any other normal day. And this time, I'm right on time. I couldn't wait to get out of the door when I awoke in the wee hours of dawn, still feeling like I was being watched.

Yesterday, the three of us managed to clean up all the mess before Ma returned from the infirmary. It would've gotten a whole lot messier if Ma came home amid all the chaos. I'm sure she gets enough of that at work. She just doesn't need the added burden on her shoulders. As much as I tell her everything about my life, there are certain events I'd rather she doesn't know, like what happened yesterday.

Both Indra and Nihal suggested that I go and report the incident to the authorities, but I just can't be bothered about it—having to wait for my turn, who knows when that'll be, and being questioned thoroughly, knowing I won't know the answers to most of them. For example, when did it happen? Do you have evidence? Around the time, where were you? Why do you think it's best for you to report? And more.

I'm getting a headache just thinking about it.

It feels like time is going painstakingly slow today. I keep counting down the hours and minutes to the bell chiming—indicating the end of the day.

Lunch, too, goes by slowly. I really am a bore to my friends throughout, only answering their questions with a yes or no. Faye doesn't eat with us. I assume that she doesn't want to be in my vicinity now. I bet even Nihal doesn't want to be anywhere near me with the state I'm currently in.

They can't blame me for acting this way. I have my moments of rudeness too. I can't pretend to smile and be happy when I'm not. Everyone has their own limits, even though they might be different. But deep down, I know I overreacted, and I have to apologize before the chasm in our friendship widens beyond saving.

"Aeni, come on!' Indra calls out to me at my working space.

'To where?'

He looks at me, 'Didn't you hear the announcement?'

I shake my head.

'What would you do without me, huh, buddy?'

We walk towards the food hall along with the rest of our classmates, who are heading in the same direction. The hall is an empty space now. All the tables and chairs have been cleared up.

I frown at the sight confronting us. There are people in military suits pacing the hall, their weapon of choice slung around their shoulders. At the end of the hall stand about thirty or more infirmary workers. They are wearing their usual white and sterile jackets and their hands are gloved in latex. They look how they usually do when prepared to go into surgery.

'What's going on?' I whisper to Indra.

In front of me, about two rows ahead, I see Faye turning around and scanning the room, as if looking for someone. She makes eye contact with me for only a second before looking ahead again. That is enough evidence to show that she is still mad at me.

'I have no idea,' Indra replies. He appears to be frowning.

Soon, everyone starts moving towards the end of the hall, heading towards the infirmary workers with syringes in their hands. Those who get injected first, don't protest—not so much as flinch. As if they've been doing this all this while, like it is a completely normal routine in our daily lives.

*I'm lost here.*

It is finally my turn, and the person who is going to put whatever substance is in the syringe inside me tells me to calm down when I start to protest and pull away. I look beside me, and Indra is just standing there. I give him a look, and he mouths the words, *'Just go with it.'*

As the needle pierces the vein in my neck and the plunger of the syringe goes down and down, I feel a new feeling. It's one that I have never experienced before. I feel as though I am being transported into a new place—a better one. One where everything becomes hazy, and it also feels as though I'm on cloud nine.

It happens all too quickly, and then the infirmary worker tells me I can go. My legs work on their own as I walk away. I don't feel anyone else around me. It's just me, alone in my own world.

Before I know it, I'm in the tram and then walking back home. I punch in the code to unlock the door and it unlocks.

*What is happening right now? Why don't I have a sense of control over my actions?*

I feel as though someone is controlling my mind and telling me what to do. I fight it off. I fight the little voice in my head.

At the same time, Ma enters the domicile, and there isn't a single expression on her face. It is as though she is expressionless and emotionless now.

I push everything away with all my might to force it to go away. I call out, 'Ma?'

She continues walking towards the kitchen and grabs a box of granola bars. She takes one out and rips off the packaging.

I stare at her in horror.

Ma never eats a granola bar. Ever. She always goes on and on about how it doesn't have the same nutrition as real food. This isn't her.

'Ma!' I call her again.

She continues chewing and swallowing her granola bar and stares at the ground. She doesn't even bother sitting down to eat. Nor does she bother about the fact that I'm here. In front of her.

Is this all being caused by what was just injected in us? And now, the substance is in my blood, my veins, my whole body? But then, how are both my mental and physical selves conscious and aware of everything that is currently happening around me?

Ma throws away the trash in the dustbin and walks towards her bedroom. I follow and scrutinize her every move. When she gets there, she goes straight to the bed, lies down on her back, and closes her eyes. She doesn't bother to take a shower or change out of her work clothes.

Something fishy is definitely going on here.

I don't know what it is. But I'm about to find out.

Soon.

# Chapter 8

I knock on Indra's bedroom window. It is the middle of the night, and I have no choice but to do this right now. I need to find out what is happening. And I need some answers. ASAP.

I hear footsteps shuffling inside, and then I see Indra's startled face staring at me from his side of the window. He looks at me with wide eyes as though he can't believe what he's seeing—that I am standing in front of him, outside his bedroom window. He rubs his eyes with the back of his hands, making sure he isn't dreaming.

I'm growing impatient, and I knock on the window again. He looks at me, and I gesture wildly at the window lock. Realization dawns on him.

He does as I tell him to, and I enter his room. I've been inside his room many times before. We used to hang out and make up our own silly games, chasing each other around the room. Those were the good times before the pull and pressure to be a functioning person in society started creeping up to us. Even before all this madness.

'What are you doing here?' Indra asks, his eyes still wide.

'I'm here to find some answers and I'm sure you'd like some too.'

'In the middle of the night? You do realize what time it is now, right? Couldn't you at least wait it out until the morning?'

I shrug and continue, 'It doesn't matter. I'm already here now.'

He raises his arms up in surrender, and I continue, 'There is seriously something wrong with what is happening to the people right now. You've seen it too.'

'Your ma went all robotic too?' he asks, a frown etched across his forehead.

'Yes.' I widen my eyes, glad to know that I am not the only one experiencing the same thing. 'For a moment, it felt like I was losing my mind. I can't explain it, but it felt like an out-of-body experience. I had no control over my body, only my mind, but I pushed it all away, and here I am now.'

'I felt it too,' Indra whispers. He stares outside, beyond the window and towards the starless sky and looks back at me. 'I felt exactly what you felt. I thought that something didn't add up and the moment whatever substance they injected in us started making me lose control, I fought it too.'

We let all the things we just said hang in the silence pervading the room.

'Do you think someone is controlling all this?' I wonder out loud.

'That seems to be the most plausible answer.' Indra rubs the back of his neck.

'Do you think it's the government? Or is it the Permaisuri? Could this be linked to what we witnessed the other day at the City Hall?' I add, voicing whatever was coming to mind.

Indra shakes his head. 'I don't know. But that's what I'd like to find out too.' He looks at me as though he can find the answers he's looking for plastered across my face, 'But why are we still in our conscious minds?'

'I don't know.' I lean back. Making my mind work twice as much is giving me a headache.

He looks to the ground. 'Right, sorry.'

I sit up straight, suddenly remembering our friends. 'Do you think Nihal and Faye are aware too?'

'I think so. Like they always say, we can always be "found together".' He does air quotes while saying the last part.

'Listen, I'm not staying long. I don't want to get caught or anything.'

'Yeah, I figured.'

'I think we should have a plan, but we should include Nihal and Faye too,' I suggest.

Indra agrees and says, 'I'm following.'

'Tomorrow morning, you find Nihal before going to the Academy, and I'll look for Faye, since I live closer to her and you to Nihal,' I explain while pacing around the room. 'If they are aware, we need to tell them to act like everybody else.'

Indra looks unsettled, seeing me pace around, going back and forth from one wall to another. He stops me by putting his arm out. 'What, like we're being controlled too?'

'Do you have a better option other than that?' I ask, eyebrow raised.

He shrugs.

I stand by my words. 'We need to do it. No, we have to. Remember what happened to my ma, someone was in her head, and I was there. It was not her voice. It was a man's.'

'Okay.' Indra still looks unsure.

'I'm sorry, but I'm just paranoid.'

'I know. I get it. I understand what you're feeling because I've seen my parents and little sister like that. There's no way I can control it or even know how to fix it. I feel helpless, and I also just want to do something but I don't know where to even begin. You get me, right?'

'Yeah, I do.'

We sit on his bed like two friends would, silently consoling each other, just deep in our own thoughts.

'Okay then,' I stand up after what felt like hours, 'I better go now.'

He nods.

I climb down from Indra's bedroom window and head back home.

* * *

I wait for Faye at the side of her domicile so no one can see me. Especially the military people. I see them roaming the streets. Still, everyone is acting as if it is another normal day in Killen when there is absolutely nothing normal about the situation.

That includes Ma. She showered this morning, changed into a new set of clothes, walked straight into the kitchen, and opened another granola bar. To me, it's not a normal day. And to whoever else is still conscious and aware of their surroundings, everything feels different and chilling to the bone.

Faye walks out of her domicile, and I quickly grab her before anyone can see us. She lets out a surprised yelp, and I have to cover her mouth before she gives us away. I look around before releasing my grip on her. 'Sorry, I had to do that.'

She looks at me, eyes roving my face tentatively. 'Aeni?'

I give her a small smile but snap out of it. To confirm that she is still herself, I ask her, 'When's my birthday?'

Faye clears her throat. 'February 6.'

'Okay, good. It is you.' I look around to make sure no one is listening. The people around pay her no mind, walking straight ahead towards their destinations.

'Listen, we don't have much time here. So, pay attention and hear what I have to say really well because I'm not repeating it.'

She nods. I tell her what I discussed with Indra in his room last night. 'We need to act like everyone else because if we get caught, who knows what will happen. You get that part now, right?'

She nods enthusiastically. 'I don't know what happened last night and even this morning but it has really scared me.'

I put my hands on her shoulders. 'Don't worry, we'll get through this together. We'll meet up with the boys at the hill after classes end to discuss what we're going to do about this situation. For now, the plan is just to blend in.'

'Sounds like a good idea.' Faye gives me a thumbs up.

We wait for a few minutes and slowly head to the tram station. I keep my eyes forward and hold my breath every time I see a military suit. Never in my life have I been so nervous around those guys. I have always respected them. From a distance.

Soon, we arrive at the Academy and head straight to the floor below and into our classroom. Indra appears and walks beside me in the corridor, giving me a thumbs up. In my peripheral view, I see Nihal just behind him. Their expressions give nothing away.

I sigh in relief, but I know that I cannot truly feel relieved and assured until all goes as per our plan, and we do not get caught. We trudge into our classroom, and I can feel, deep inside me, that something strange is about to happen.

PART II

# Chapter 9

'If it isn't you, Ahmad!' It's Rat Guy. Yes, that's what we decided to call him, since we are not on first name basis with each other. Plus, he kind of has the same features as a rat.

Have I mentioned who he is yet? He is the same man who gave me my aptitude test back in Secondary, and the other teacher who teaches us for our practical. Why is it him today? I am not in the mood as it is, but now he shows up? I am not happy about this.

The anger that I'm containing inside me has to be tempered down as he is standing so close to me. His disgusting breath makes me want to barf right then.

I stare ahead, pretending like a robot, and unfortunately, I get a glimpse at his spiteful face and cringe inwardly. How does he manage to look more and more like a rat with each passing day? I swear, even his skin is turning greyish.

I feel so bad for him sometimes, but then I think about all the bad things that he has said to others and how hurtful they have been. No, he deserves to look like that. No offence to rats because, honestly, he isn't even worthy of being compared to a stray rat.

'Come closer! I won't bite,' he says.

I swear, I could have killed him right at that moment. The consequences are holding me back.

I might even get shipped off to the Remote Island where they took the mother and her children.

He walks from the front of the practical classroom and slowly makes his way over to my table. 'It's great to see you like this, unaware of your surroundings. Best of all, I get to say whatever I like and not get a single response from you.'

A table away, I catch Indra twitching and hope he contains his anger too. I can't see Nihal from my spot, and everyone else is unperturbed. I do my best to remain unfazed by his words, maintaining my façade.

'Tsk tsk!' He stares at me from top to bottom. He lowers his voice, 'You have always reminded me of your father during our time in the Academy. He was wild, reckless, a rebel, and thought so highly of himself. Yes, your father and I are the same age and went here together twenty years ago. Truly, blood does run thicker than water and you both disgust me. I never knew what your mother saw in your father. She should have known better than to get involved with him.'

I'd say that my dad is a million times better and worth so much more than this Rat Guy in front of me. No, *he disgusts me!*

He continues with his spiteful words, 'For years, I have planned my revenge. It is the most brilliant plan. You should have seen it, it is absolutely remarkable. It is the kind of plan that can cause war to erupt in the city. I spent days and nights awake, perfecting my work of art. Wait, why am I telling you all this? You probably can't hear me as dumb as you are.'

He smirks and turns around to walk away. I give him the most hateful and angry expression. As though he felt it, he suddenly stops mid-walk. My face has been a blank mask, and he looks at me disgustedly. *Well, you know what? You and I are the same because you disgust me too*, I wanted to say to him.

'Oh, and Ahmad? I was there when your father was killed. I was in the same room as him, breathing the same air as him. I know you'd be so giddy if you knew or heard anything about him, since you were so little back then to even understand what happened and what was going on. What a shame you are, Ahmad. What a shame that you are the result of a beautiful vixen and an absolute scum.'

He laughs evilly before murmuring to himself, 'She deserved so much better than him.'

He walks out of the classroom and leaves us to fend for ourselves. As soon as Rat Guy is out the door and some distances away, I quickly walk out of the room and go to the bathroom before I explode. Rage and anger consume me. They will consume every part of me if I don't get out of here fast enough.

I enter a bathroom stall and heave all the contents of my stomach out. There goes all of my breakfast. I stare at myself in the mirror, my face pale from hearing the harsh truth that came out of the Rat Guy's mouth—it is staring right back at me.

*Was everything he said the truth?* I don't know what to even believe anymore. Ma told me that my father died on duty protecting Killen, as it was his mission. He was an army officer, who started off as a soldier and climbed his way up to the top. I heard that he was a commander who accidentally led his comrade astray due to a miscommunication. But what if that isn't the truth? Why would he be brutally murdered? Did he commit a felony—an injustice?

I put a hand over my mouth to muffle my frustrated scream and fall to my knees. My head is pounding and everything is starting to get blurry and out of proportion.

I hear the door being opened, and I am already deliriously out of this world. I hear someone calling my name in the distance.

I feel my shoulders being shaken and my head lolls to the side. 'Aeni!'

Is this the end? Is this how people feel when they are dying? I'll gladly embrace death if it'll stop the pain I'm feeling.

I feel a stinging slap across my right cheek and see the tiled floor slowly emerge into my field of vision. I can see everything clearly now.

'Aeni! Wake up!'

I look up and Indra's worried face is inches from mine. I lightly shove him aside to give me some space, and his shoulders slump in relief. 'Aeni? Are you okay?'

'I think so,' I whisper in response, my voice raspy and parched from throwing up. 'I don't know what came over me.'

'You're lucky that I'm the one who found you in this state first. Or else, all sorts of trouble would've been coming your way.'

My eyebrows furrow, 'Wait, how did you know I was here?'

'I saw you running away out of the workspace, and I followed you here.'

I look around at my surroundings, as if to confirm, and stare at him in horror. 'And you just walked inside the girl's washroom? Get out! Go before someone sees you.'

'I had no choice. I had to follow you and warn you not to act out of the ordinary. To blend in and act like everyone else.'

I sigh as I lean my head back against the cold wall. Who knows what would have happened to me if it was someone else. I don't even want to think about it. I'm just glad, end of discussion.

He places his hands on my shoulders. 'Are you really okay, though? You look really shaken up.'

'I'm fine. Or I will be once I forget about this. That is, if I can stop thinking about it.' I close my eyes and try to push all the words that were revealed to me not long ago.

'What are you talking about? What happened back there? What did the Rat Guy say to you?' He actually looks worried.

I open my eyes and stare at the ceiling, 'Nothing much. I just wasn't feeling well, that's all.'

For some reason, I don't want to share this new-found information that I've received with Indra or anyone else. Not even my ma, especially not with her, since she could have a breakdown. This could be the one and only time I'll ever know and hear anything about my late dad. Ma has always been so discreet and secretive about him. She acts as though the only memories she has of him shouldn't be jinxed by even mentioning him. To her, my dad is like a cracked glass that can shatter because of a single touch.

Indra still looks unconvinced but decides better than to push me and starts to get up off the cold floor. 'We should probably go now.'

I take a deep breath, willing myself to find my strength before nodding at Indra. 'Let's go.'

We quickly make our way to our designated stations and spend the rest of the day as normally as we can. Fortunately, Rat Guy never came back to the classroom. I lock eyes with Nihal, who is a few tables behind me and giving me a concerned look, and assure him with a small smile. Every once in a while, I sneak glances at others around me to see their reactions and any particular actions. They all never take a break, they don't say anything, and not so much as blink. They're like robots, living off some sort of unidentifiable energy.

I can't even take a break to calm down and take a breather, since everyone is doing their work. Everyone has been assigned to finish up their task like there's no tomorrow.

On my way out of the Academy, Indra slips a note in my hand. Inside, he's asked me to meet at our usual hangout place on the hill. I calmly take a few steps away from him to make sure no one notices before subtly taking a turn to the back of the building that leads straight to the bottom of the hill.

The four of us have set up our own trail, since heading up to the actual place can get complicated and lead to someone easily getting lost. But we remember the route, including every plant situated along the way, like the back of our hands.

When I reach our own little nook on the hill, I see my friends huddling close to each other. Aside from our domicile and Pak Mat's mamak place, this is mostly where we can be found. I really can't remember when we discovered this place, but I do know why we choose to hang out here. It's because the place has an aura of tranquillity none of the other places in Killen can offer. Or maybe there are more places like this one outside the Central Island, but us commoners aren't allowed to leave this one. Only those who have been granted permission for a very specific reason can leave.

Killen is a very strict city to live in. It's probably the main reason why I've always wondered how the outside world is like. Do they live under a monarchy? Are there cities like Killen? What do they eat? How does anything work out there?

Snapping out of my thoughts, I quickly make my way over to my friends and sit down, sandwiched between the boys. 'Are we coming up with the plan now?'

'Yes,' Indra answers with a serious look on his face.

'I'm still so confused with everything that has happened in the past few days and is still happening right now. Ever since Ma went completely still . . .' I'm gazing at the sky as I say this.

'Well, Aeni, you're not the only one who feels that way.' Nihal stretches his long legs out and sighs. 'We're all just as confused as you are.'

'So . . . are we just going to continue pretending to be like everyone else?' Faye wonders. 'It doesn't feel right for us to do that, in my opinion.'

'Then do you suggest we report and turn ourselves in?' Indra looks at her incredulously.

'It might sound like a bad idea right now but try to think about it, it's the most sensible thing to do. It's the right thing to do.' Faye defends herself while stating her argument.

'But we don't know what they'll do to us when we turn ourselves in. They could act too fast and we'll end up just like everyone else—controlled like robots,' Indra voices his concerns.

'It is still the right thing to do,' Faye continues to stand by her opinion.

'On this, I'm going to have to agree with Indra,' I step into the conversation.

'You always agree with Indra. We get it, you two are best friends. Yadda yadda yadda.' Nihal rolls his eyes.

'If we turn ourselves in, though, not only will they discover this place, our spot, but also who knows what'll happen to our fates? We might even be sentenced to leave Central Island for Linggi. Everyone knows how spooky and haunting that place is. I've heard that every time someone new lands their feet on the island, a new nightmare unleashes. Whatever happens, I'm going to turn a blind eye and stick with the plan. This might just be a phase and everyone will be themselves again soon.'

'But we don't know when that'll be!' Faye bursts out. She turns to Nihal, hoping that he'll take her side. 'What do you have to say about all of this?'

He's staring at the ground. We all think he is going to ignore us when he finally says, 'I agree with them.'

He points to me and Indra.

Faye looks at him with the utmost betrayal plastered across her face. 'Nihal . . . I . . . but you . . .'

He still refuses to look her in the eye and shrugs. 'I think they're right about it. The point now is to dodge the bullet, since that is our main concern and I think that this is the best idea to dodge the said bullet.'

'But it isn't right.' Faye looks at each of us as if she cannot believe that we are her friends who have been standing with each other ever since we were little and faced whatever obstacles have come our way together, always.

'You guys are making a mistake about this.' She stands up like she can't stand being in our presence anymore. 'You're wrong. You will see that you're wrong.'

I watch her go as she treks down the trail until she is long gone. She's acting so strange and so out of the ordinary. It's like Faye is no longer herself.

# Chapter 10

That night, my mind is swarming with so many things that I can't even shut it down to sleep. I toss and turn on my bed, trying to block it but barely managing to keep it all away—it refuses to leave me. Suddenly, sleep becomes a luxury that I can't quite reach. It's close, but I just can't make myself reach it. I'm growing tired of all this. Things have just been going awry. *Why can't things be the way they used to be?* That's probably just wishful thinking.

I sit up and stare out the window at the sky, which seems as starless as my soul. No one knows what happened to the stars, only that they seem to have vanished into thin air. No one can give a valid reason why, not even the scientists.

The whole night, I sit there, motionless, and before I know it, the sun replaces the moon, and the cycle continues for a few days. Faye continues to keep a distance from us. Even when we bump into her, she heads in the other direction, like we're some sort of disease that she's desperate to steer clear of. I keep snoozing away in my own seat as sleep relentlessly continues to stay away from me at night.

My spirits have been dashing to an all-time low with each passing day. Apart from my friends, everyone else remains still and lifeless. I can't stand looking at my ma not being her lively self, so whenever I'm back at our domicile, I lock myself in my room. A part of me even hopes that Ma would barge in but she never does. She's not herself anymore.

One night, I'm lying down on my bed with a million thoughts running around when I hear a tap on my window. It's already past midnight, and no one is supposed to be outside their domicile after curfew. I hurry over to my window. Nihal is waiting outside for me.

I slide the window open, 'What are you doing here at this hour? You should be back in your own domicile.'

'We need to talk,' he says like it is a casual thing to do and that it won't totally be breaking the rules if one of the army officers find him out here.

'Talk about what?' My eyebrows furrow. *Has he lost his mind?*

But considering I just did the same thing a few days ago, I'm in no situation to admonish him about this.

'Just come out. We'll wait.'

I was about to ask who 'we' refers to, but of course, it's Indra. Who else would it be?

I grab a sweatshirt and put it on over my T-shirt. I quietly and cautiously tiptoe around the living area and make my way outside, where the boys are waiting for me.

'What's going on?' I ask them.

Nihal looks resigned. 'Don't ask us, it was Faye who set up this meeting and wants to meet us all. She asked us to meet her at the hill in thirty minutes. This happened twenty minutes ago. We need to get going. We don't want to keep her waiting now, do we? You guys know better than to face her wrath.'

'It's not like she's not mad at you, too, because she is. We all contributed in pissing her off.' Indra tries to defend himself to no avail.

'There's no use arguing about it now. The thing is we are all at fault here, and we need to go and meet her right now.' I sigh. We should never have turned against one another. Times like this is when we need to stick together the most. Who knows what'll even happen in the future. What if this isn't just a phase and something that'll continue to happen forever? I shudder at the thought.

It takes us longer than usual to get there, since we can't ride on the tram. It stops running after 10.00 p.m. and begins operating again in the morning at 6.00. Luckily, since we took a shortcut through alleyways, we did not pass any patrolling military officers.

We arrive at the hill without much time to spare. Beside the clearing, we see a lone figure standing—waiting. She turns around in our direction and offers us a small smile.

I can't explain why, but I feel despondent seeing Faye, as though I can feel that the reason behind her asking us to come here is something bad.

'Thanks for taking the time to meet me here.'

'Faye, we're sorry. We shouldn't have—'

'Don't worry about it. I'm sure you had your reasons,' she cuts Indra off.

He persists, 'But still—'

Faye takes a few steps towards him and looks at each one of us. 'Listen, I didn't set this up expecting an apology from the three of you, but I think that we shouldn't prolong this any longer. We're friends, right?'

'Of course, we're friends,' Nihal assures her. Indra and I nod resolutely in response.

Nihal's statement makes Faye smile. I'm glad about that. We all are. But it still doesn't add up, the fact why she has gathered us all here tonight.

'But why did you want to meet us tonight? You do realize that we're breaking the rules, right?' Nihal is hoping for a reaction out of Faye, but she just smiles.

'I know that, but I have to say what I'm about to when the four of us are by ourselves, so that no one else can eavesdrop on our conversation.'

'But how can you be certain of others listening in on our conversation when they're acting like robots, untethered from any human emotions?'

She looks at me, and her gaze doesn't stray away, 'What makes you think that they can't hear you just because they're being controlled? After all, we must always be cautious about everything we do now. You don't know it, but there could be someone out there who is watching us.'

'What do you mean by that? Is someone actually watching us then?' Shivers suddenly run down my spine, knowing that someone is keeping tabs on my every move.

'I can't exactly say,' Faye looks away.

'Do you know something that we don't?' I look at Faye in a different light. Could she have discovered something and not told us about it? That hurts me. I thought we're best friends who tell each other everything.

'It's almost like you're trying to make us read between the lines,' Indra suggests, figuring out where my point is coming from. Nihal remains silent, looking at each of us every time we say something.

Faye shakes her head, looking dejected. She murmurs to herself, 'No, it's . . . I . . .'

I come closer to her, gritting my teeth as I try to understand what she's getting at. 'You what?' I ask softly.

Faye shakes her head again, keeping her gaze fixed on the ground. Finally, in a low voice, she whispers, 'I . . . It's nothing.'

It's like she's speaking in riddles, and I feel frustrated about it. I know I can't get through to her right now. The only thing I can do is wait for her to open up to us about whatever it is that's got her acting like this.

A wind blows, and we hear weird noises coming from every direction around us. I think we've all started to feel a little chill in our bones.

'We should probably head back home before we get caught.' Faye suggests, looking worriedly at our surroundings.

'Don't jinx it by saying it out loud or it'll actually happen.' Nihal looks around nervously.

Indra rolls his eyes. 'You're just being paranoid.'

'Who cares if I am? Let's just go back.' Nihal walks a few steps ahead and gestures for us to follow him.

Faye keeps trying to gain my attention, and I cave in. I give her a nod in acknowledgement and nothing else. There's still something that makes me suspicious of her.

I quickly walk away and join Indra as we slowly trek down the hill. In the midst of it, we manage to get ourselves involved in a race to see who'll reach the bottom first. If I am currently in my right mind, I'll say that we're being ridiculous, but I'm not. I don't know if I even want to be.

I laugh at Indra as he stumbles and tumbles down when we've almost reached the finishing line. It feels so good to just let go and laugh for a bit. It feels like a momentary relief. Faye, who is right behind me, shakes her head in disbelief.

'Wait, stop,' I say. I stop mid-run, making Faye bump into my back and a few revolting words escape her mouth.

'What's wrong?' Faye asks.

'What's going on? We need to get going and be in our own respective domiciles, right now!' Nihal says, clearly getting impatient—and maybe a little paranoid?

I shush them.

'That's really rude.' Nihal mutters.

I wave my hand in front of his face to shut him up before someone hears and finds us, maybe he just didn't get it the first time around.

'Seriously, what—' I place my hand on Nihal's mouth to silence him. He just can't shut up, can he? Even at a crucial moment like this I still have to tell him countless times to be silent.

'Go back and hide.' I motion for them to turn around, and they all obligingly comply with my sudden demand.

We all seek refuge in a dark alley between two stores that are now closed for business since we're out here in the middle of the night. We are accompanied by nothing but our fearful expectations.

'I think the coast is clear now,' I say after a while.

'What the hell is going on, Aeni?' Faye asks.

'There are guards surrounding that building and a car parked in front of the Academy.' I point towards the Academy.

'A car? Are you serious?'

We're fascinated by the mere thought of cars because we know that only someone from the highest hierarchy would ever use a car. And the whole nation has never met Permaisuri's helpers or the rulers alongside her, maybe she rules Killen all on her own, we don't know. They keep everything confidential up there and leave us hanging.

It makes me wonder, *What else are they hiding from us?*

'Why would someone important come here, to visit the Academy? At this hour?' Nihal wonders out loud.

The rest of us look dumbfounded.

'I have no idea but something very suspicious is either about to happen or has already happened,' I state. 'But whatever it is, I think we should get back home. Now.'

* * *

I open the front door and close it behind me as quietly as possible. Ma is probably still out of it, but I am careful anyway as a precaution.

Her bedroom door creaks, and I stare at her seemingly lifeless form on the bed, her chest rising up and down is the only indication of life. Only her body seems to be alive while her consciousness is nowhere to be found. The clock ticks away, and I step closer towards her. I watch her sleep, transported back in time to when I was a little girl. It was a habit of mine to watch her when I couldn't sleep. Only this time, it feels different.

I wish that I was still a girl in the warm embrace of her ma who loves her with all her heart and knows that she, too, feels the same way.

# Chapter 11

I'm being kicked, and moments later, someone steps on my torso. I yelp in pain. Ma, who is the culprit, falls down, pulls herself right back up, and resumes her daily routine.

I don't know how I'm even supposed to react to that.

During the wee hours of the morning, I dozed off on the floor beside ma's bed until the moon was replaced by the sun.

She is still in her robotic trance as she makes her way out of the room, and I hear the bathroom door close.

*Who is doing this? And what's their motive? Is there a hidden agenda?* I have so many questions and I'm frustrated that no one will answer them. My mind feels suffocated, and I feel that I am constantly in distress. I hate this feeling. I hate everything. I never thought I'd say this, but I need my ma back. I need her to warm me with her smile that could win a hundred men's hearts. She doesn't realize this but she always knows the right thing to say on every occasion.

I want her back.

I sit on the floor until she steps out of the bathroom and heads to the kitchen. I don't need to observe her to know where exactly she is at what time.

7.00 a.m.: wake up

7.20 a.m.: get out of the shower

7.25 a.m.: breakfast, which only consists of a granola bar and a glass of water

7.30 a.m.: go to work

7.00 p.m.: come back home

7.10 p.m.: shower

7.30 p.m.: dinner

8.00 p.m.: sleep

And the cycle has been continuing to this day. I am so sick of it. I want it to stop. I want things to go back to the way they were before.

The doorbell breaks me out of my stupor, but I'm too tired to move. I stay where I am. I wish that I could just stay here, but I know that it'll only raise suspicions. We're already in trouble for not being like everyone else—unalive, robotic, and mindless beings.

'Aeni! Open up! I know you're in there!' Indra bangs on the door.

I slowly make my way to the door while Indra, being the impatient person he is, continues banging the door.

'Aeni! If you don't open up the door this instance, I will—'

His fist hangs in mid-air as I yank the door open. I give him a bored look. 'What will you do? Punch me? Report me to the authorities? Huh, what will you do?'

He ignores what I just said and looks at me from top to bottom. 'What are you doing? Why are you still not dressed?'

'I was preoccupied.' This is a total lie, but he doesn't need to know that.

'What the hell, Aeni? You know that by this time you should already be on your way to the Academy.'

I shrug, 'Yeah, sure.'

'What has gotten into you? Why are you making me worry about you?' He sighs, looking defeated by my appearance. 'Look, I know you're mad and upset about this whole situation—we all are. But that doesn't mean you can just act however the hell you want. You need to get it together or we're all going to be in a heap of trouble.'

I ignore him. I am fully aware of everything he's said, and I am not proud of it. I will do better, I promise.

Before I can say anything, I look up in surprise as Faye comes running in our direction. She has to catch her breath and is panting when she finally reaches us.

'We . . . everyone . . . City Hall . . .'

'Talk properly. In complete sentences,' Indra emphasizes.

'Take your time, tell us slowly,' I say, reassuring her. What she has to say seems really important, so I wait eagerly.

She's still catching her breath as we stare at each other and then at her in anticipation. Indra's lips are set in a thin line, and I know that he's just patiently waiting.

'There's a . . . the Permaisuri is at the City Hall for an impromptu visit, and everyone is there right now as we speak.' A look of utter surprise is plastered across my face as she adds, 'We need to go—like, now! Right now!'

I nod, but apparently, none of my synapses are responding. What's going on? I really hope it's nothing bad.

'What the hell are you waiting for? We need to go *now*!' Faye makes a hurrying motion. 'We'll be in trouble if someone notices we're not there.'

We don't linger any longer. I step out of the domicile and close the door behind me. We rush to the tram station and when we board the tram, we're the only passengers. Deep down, I'm telling myself not to start freaking out and to stay calm—everything is going to be all right.

*It's going to be okay*, I hope.

'The next stop is Central Station. Alight here for the City Hall, the Academy, and the Hub.'

When the doors of the tram slide open, we cautiously step out. Glancing left and right to look out for anyone. Or one of the army officers stationed outside. I sigh in relief as I don't spot anyone there. We quietly exit the station and walk the short distance to the City Hall, where I can see figures of all ages and colours, staring straight ahead, their complete attention on the stage. Everything is quiet. Even the black-clothed army officers are standing still in a specific stance. None are pacing with their guns slung over their shoulders. All of them are standing still while clutching the guns pressed against their chests.

*I do not have a good feeling about any of this.*

Why is the Permaisuri here? It's not even time for her to deliver her quarterly speech. She's standing at the edge of the stage in her maroon cloak, which splits down the middle. Usually, she goes straight to the podium, scrutinizes each one of us, and begins her speech. But I can tell that this time, it's different. I don't even know what I see as odd anymore because it has been occurring in front of me on a daily basis.

We slip into the crowd, and I give my full attention to the Permaisuri. She's just standing there and not even scrutinizing the citizens. She's looking up at the sky, the floor, and then the people who are all there standing and staring at her. I hide behind a tall man as I follow her every move.

Finally, after what feels like hours, a man walks up to her, looking serious. They're talking in hushed tones, the creases on Permaisuri's eyebrows indicate that they might be having a heated discussion.

I take a peep at my friends—we have decided to scatter around instead of being in one place, so that we may see the event unfold from every angle. Obviously, I'm dying to talk to them about the situation at hand, but it'll give me away, and I'm smarter than to go down that path.

The Permaisuri starts taking a few steps backwards, the frown still evident on her face, and shoves the man aside. He is blocking her way but she sidesteps him and storms away. The man continues standing there for a few moments, looks around the crowd as though assessing the citizens, and then firmly walks away.

*What just happened? Did I seriously just witness that?* I feel like I'm going crazy. Can everything just stop and go back to how it was? I know I've said that so many times in my mind, I've lost count, but it has now become a necessity to me, like breathing.

When everyone is forming a straight line and filing out of the City Hall heading to their respective domiciles, I have to stop myself from bolting away. I can feel Indra's presence behind me—he's doubting my ability to make any necessary decision. We board the tram and when I see no hint of military officers, only the still and stiff beings around us, I slump to the floor like I've given up on life and everything it has to offer. I don't even feel faint, but here I am anyway, pretending to be just that. Am I being too dramatic?

'Aeni!' Indra pushes my body sideways so that I am lying flat on my back on the floor. His face is conveying utter panic and horror. I feel bad for pulling such a stunt. Now that I've thought over what I just did, I feel like hiding myself away from civilization. Behind him, Nihal is looking at me nervously, like I might collapse again, while Faye has a disgruntled look and I don't know how to comprehend that.

I sit up. 'I'm fine. I don't know what came over me.'

'Are you sure? Do you need to go to the infirmary?' Nihal offers.

Indra replies on my behalf before I can say anything, 'Do you want us to get caught? Can you please think before you say something? Nihal, I swear. You really must think first.'

'I'm fine.' I reassure him. 'I think I just need to lie down and catch up on some sleep. I think I'm just sleep deprived. I haven't been able to sleep lately, ever since all this started.'

'Right. The moment when it all started,' Faye says, staring into the distance, looking troubled by what I just said, before continuing, 'when was that exactly?'

'You know when.' Nihal gives her a funny look. 'You're really acting weird lately. Is there anything you'd like to tell us? My gut keeps telling me that you're hiding something from us. I don't know what it is, but I'd really like to know.'

'What do you mean?' She tilts her head to the right a little, and at her words, the three of us take a few steps back. Yes, Faye may be the smartest out of us all, but she never talks the way she just did a second ago. She sounds wiser and nothing like herself. She usually looks strong yet has a softness to her, but looking at her now, I don't find a trace of it at all.

'Faye,' I start, voice trembling. I really hope my assumptions are wrong and the person standing in front of me is the friend I've known ever since we were children. She locks her eyes on me, which look almost sinister. 'Where do we usually hang out?'

She smiles. 'Our domiciles, of course.'

I stop short. My assumption was right after all. *This is definitely not Faye.*

'Who are you and what have you done to our friend?' Nihal yells out while holding her by her shoulders and shaking her.

I grab his forearm and yank him away from Faye. 'Calm down, Nihal. This is not the time to be emotional.'

'Who are you? Tell us what you want!' Indra demands. He's looking at his friend as though he no longer knows who she is.

Faye, looking nonchalant, snickers and smiles. We take a few steps back at the sight. She looks as though she's thinking of murdering us, and the thought is exciting her.

*What is going on?*

'You have committed treason, and you will pay for it. Our commander will capture you soon,' the sinister smile is back. 'Then you'll be sorry.'

'If there's no one here to act against whoever this is, everyone's too much of a sissy to punch her in the face, I will,' Nihal says, ready to bring his friend down. He sounds adamant and headstrong, as if he made up his mind ages ago.

'Are you crazy? That's our friend. She's still Faye, but it seems like someone has temporarily taken over her body.' Indra looks at both of them in horror. Then, he continues, 'Aeni, stop him. This is madness.'

'The only thing that is madness here is the fact that we are not doing anything about this. She just said we've committed treason. I have absolutely no idea as to why we have been accused of such a thing. What I do know is that we have been falsely accused. They could think we are just a bunch of teenagers who think we can take over Killen with our rebelliousness. And I think they're delusional because we are just as clueless as everyone else here,' Nihal rambles, looking as lost as ever.

'I have to agree with him on this,' I say looking at Indra, who is speechless after hearing Nihal's words. If we weren't in such a confusing situation, I'd be so proud of him, but things can't always happen the way we expect them to.

Faye snickers again, and we look at her. 'Falsely accused, huh? A bunch of teenagers who think they can take over Killen with their rebelliousness. You have got to be kidding me right now! Treason is still treason whether it is deliberate or not.'

'Shut up, you imbecile! Leave us alone! You have no right to do this.' Nihal is not done. He remains headstrong and unwilling to back down.

And for the second time, I beg Nihal, 'Calm down! Keep your emotions in check!'

'You're right, I don't,' Faye responds to Nihal in a man's voice. The voice is hoarse, like he hasn't had a drink of water for a very long time. 'But it'll change soon enough because I will have the authority and take over the throne, which has always been mine to begin with. And when that happens, I will act however I wish to. Very soon.'

It's a voice that I record and store at the back of my mind. The words haunt me, and I keep going back to them again and again.

The doors of the tram open and an announcement blasts throughout the vehicle: 'Alight here for the domiciles.'

Faye slumps to the floor, and we just stand there in the middle of the tram. Everyone else gets off the vehicle. As the tram rolls away from our stop, it's just us inside now.

# Chapter 12

'What happened?' Faye asks groggily as she clutches her head and sits up. 'Why the hell am I on the floor?'

'You tell me,' Nihal says dejectedly and collapses on the seat in relief. 'I'm so glad you're back.'

'What's going on?' She hoists herself up and takes a seat beside Nihal.

'We're still trying to figure that part out,' I say, relieved to see my friend being herself again. Even though Ma still probably is not. I keep my tears at bay and look out of the window, taking in the sights of our city as the tram passes by.

'Can someone please tell me what the hell just happened and stop talking in riddles? I already have a headache.' She tries to stand up, but she must be dizzy because she sways. Indra, being closest to her, helps her up and guides her to a seat. She rubs her temples. 'Wait, weren't we already at the City Hall? Why are we heading there again?'

'Where do you want us to start?' Indra asks, looking worried.

She leans back on the seat and closes her eyes. 'Just tell me what happened.'

We begin to tell her exactly what happened. We start with what happened at the City Hall and end with where we are now—without missing anything. We even tell her what happened from each of our perspectives.

She takes a moment to take it all in. 'I can't believe this. This is just madness.'

'That's exactly what we said,' Indra states, nodding in agreement.

'Thank you for not punching me in the face, Nihal. Even though I probably deserved it,' Faye jokes to lighten the mood.

Faye musters a smile. 'Can't deny that I would have been tempted to do the same if I was in your situation.'

'So, what do we do now?' Faye asks the question that we're all wondering about.

*What happens now?*

'Guys,' Nihal is looking at the ceiling, and I can't help but wonder what he's staring at, 'could it be possible that we're being monitored, and they can listen to our conversations, just like Faye said last night?'

'What are you talking about now?' Indra says, sounding confused.

'I know that's what I said last night, but I didn't think it was really happening. I was just saying that as a hunch, that's all. In fact, I don't even know how they can be monitoring us. I don't know how they can do that,' Faye adds honestly.

Nihal looks excited as he says, 'Maybe they are monitoring us through the people they are controlling? Like they have planted a micro camera in their eyes and—'

'Guys!' Something caught my eye and I called out to get their attention. 'Look, over there!'

I point at a surveillance video monitor. As we stare at it, we reckon with the possibility that our cover might be blown. We are screwed! I know that's what we're all thinking about right now.

*Busted!*

'We need to get off at the next stop.' Indra is the first to speak up—always dependable and offering the most plausible course of action.

'But what if they're already there, waiting with rifles pointed at our heads?' Nihal exclaims in horror.

'Say goodbye to freedom!' Faye says, her face serious.

'We're definitely going to be sent off to that nightmare of an island to rot there, that's for sure.' Indra joins them.

'This wouldn't have happened if you guys would've just confessed to the authorities.'

The last line comes from Faye and both Nihal and Indra, who are full of rage, spew out sentences that make absolutely no sense to me.

*I've had enough.*

'SHUT UP!' I scream. I am then greeted with stunned silence. 'Stop bickering. We need a plan.'

'But plans don't always work out the way we want them to,' Indra states. 'Look what's happening now when we followed your so-called plan to pretend as if we are like everyone else!'

'Hey! I thought that was the best thing to do. At least we knew how to deal with the situation and be calm about it at the time,' I defend myself. I feel betrayed that Indra of all people has decided to blame this on me. Is it my fault that the plan didn't work out?

'Yeah, well we still could have dealt with it differently,' Indra points out.

'You didn't say anything when I suggested the plan. You could have come up with a better idea then, maybe, we wouldn't be here right now, arguing when we should be teaming up together and figuring out what to do next.' I rub my arms as if to soothe the anger burning inside me.

Indra is about to argue, but Faye stops him, 'Enough! We get it. You guys are both upset, but this isn't the time. You two are giving me a headache. We're nearly approaching the next station, and we need to move.'

As if on cue, the announcement blares out of the speakers: 'The next stop is Central Station. Alight here for the City Hall, the Academy, and the Hub.'

I'm tired of arguing and looking at the expressions on my friends' faces—they feel the same way.

With a resolute nod, I determinedly exclaim, 'Whatever happens, we'll fight together. But if you're not with me, say it now, and we can part ways.'

Nihal and Faye give me a nod while Indra pretends to be interested in his shoes. I ignore him and take it as a sign that he's also with us. We wait for the doors to open as the tram slows down and then comes to a complete halt. We can't make ourselves look out the window so, instead, we just go with whatever awaits us at the station.

The doors open, and we slowly turn around. The sight that greets us could bring tears to my eyes. I am not even ashamed to admit that. I have never felt any happier than what I feel right now. Citizens of Killen are waiting outside to board the tram, and they're all alive and well. Children are talking jovially to their parents and siblings. The grown-ups are acting like they always do. Some are scrutinizing people, some look bored, and there are a variety of other facial expressions I can find. These people are themselves again. They're acting on their own accord.

'Faye?' Mr Li calls out to his daughter, who is standing in the front row to board the tram. 'What are you doing here?'

She runs out and engulfs her baba in a big hug. I scan the scene for my ma, softly pushing everyone aside so there is enough space for me to walk around while looking for my most favourite face of all.

'Ma?'

*Is she here? Where is she?*

'Has anyone seen my ma?' I'm starting to panic even though I have no reason to. There are a lot of people here, she's probably around somewhere. I leave my friends behind and continue my search.

There's a bench on the station, and I stand on it to look for Ma. I want to yell out her name, but I hate the attention it'll bring me and the effects that'll have. People are already starting to give me weird looks, and I'm trying hard to contain my annoyance.

'Aeni!' Indra has his arms up and is waving them around to grab my attention.

I jump down the bench and make my way to him. I probably should have informed one of them first before storming off to look for Ma.

'I was off to look for my ma. Sorry I just—'

'Look, I know you really want to look for her now, but we need to go!' he cuts me off.

I look at him in alarm and, most probably, confusion. 'What do you mean we have to go?'

'Someone is looking for us.' He gives me a look of pity. Even he doesn't get to see his family in this crowd. There are way too many people and so little time for us to make a move before we are discovered.

The stubborn side of me is relentless and tries to argue even though its fruitless. I decide to try anyway to just get a glimpse of the woman who raised me. 'And how do you know that they're here to look for us? What if they're just doing their regular jobs?'

'And what if their regular jobs involve capturing us?' Indra is starting to look annoyed, but I just won't let it happen. I refuse to give up the search for Ma just yet. I have to see her. I need to see her.

Wherever she is, if she is out there, I know that she would want to see me too.

'Indra, look we don't know for sure—'

'Oh yes! We do know!' he pauses, catches his breath, and looks like he's going to slap me in the face—hard. After taking a few calming breaths, he looks at me and says, 'Aeni, we don't have time for you to be stupid right now. Nor do we have the time to be having this conversation. There are soldiers right behind us, and they look as though they're looking for us as we speak. Get down.'

I crouch behind two old ladies who are as clueless as two old ladies can be. And true enough, just as Indra said, there are two soldiers scanning faces and walking around like they are on a mission—to look for us. Traitors, rebels, and whatever else they wish to call us.

My heart beats louder. I do not like to be in this situation. At all.

'We need to go!' Indra whispers in panic.

I nod and as we are about to walk away, we hear one of the old ladies scream, 'Stop right there, you two youngsters!'

Everyone turns their heads to look our way and, once again, all of their attention is on us.

I suddenly feel so naked.

'Capture them!'

It is true, then. They are out looking for us and hoping to capture us after all. I had my hopes up for nothing.

We run like our lives depend on it, which in that exact moment, is definitely true. Not only are the two old ladies trying to catch us—which might I add they are failing at miserably, since their muscles seem to be failing them—but so, too, are the rest of the citizens. The situation feels as though we are being chased around by zombies.

I don't understand what the hell is going on right now, and I don't let my mind comprehend the situation. The only thing I need to do now is run as fast as I can and hope no one catches up to me.

A little girl comes in my way, and I wish for her to stop. She looks like a really sweet little girl, but then she starts screaming this bloodcurdling scream that reverberates throughout the station and gone is the image of the sweet little girl she was before. She looks demented, and it creeps me out. She doesn't stop and continues to jump on my back, and I move around sideways to make her release me. Her grasp on me becomes tighter, and it feels like a death grip.

Who knew a little innocent and sweet girl like her could act so savage? This poor girl, she probably won't have a future with the way she's acting right now but who cares about that right now? Not me, definitely.

She makes a growling noise and, like a dog, tries to bite me. I don't think twice when I grab her hands and slam her on the ground. I want to apologize and tell her how awful I feel for doing that to her, but she doesn't even look fazed, cranes her neck, and runs towards me.

I keep running and running, shoving people around me as I go. Beside me, Indra has just punched an old man who was walking with a stick, and even in that chaotic moment, I give him an are-you-serious look and in return he looks at me like *what was I to do?*

I can't help myself, the dude just punched an old man! Poor guy.

We quickly run out of the station, and I realize that it might not be the best idea. If we go straight towards the City Hall, it'll be an open space and has a good vantage point from above. Whoever might be on a tall building could get a real shot at us for sure. The next option is to head to the market. The narrow alleys can make a great hiding place.

I don't need to tell Indra out loud for him to know where we're heading.

'Should we split up?' he yells out.

I am out of breath and ready to take a seat somewhere. I am so tired as it is that he does not need to ask me a dumb question. I holler, 'Of course not! Are you crazy?'

He, too, doesn't think that he can argue with an angry and tired version of me, so he gives up. 'Fine. See that alley?'

He points to a dark and narrow alley that I would never enter even during daylight. I nod anyway.

I enter the alley first and Indra follows suit behind me. The citizens don't stop. I just wonder what kind of energy they have. They show no signs of stopping or even any sign that they're tired. I wish they would, even if it was for a little while. Even some of the older ones don't look tired, their minor weakness is that they only walk slower than the rest.

It is dark in here and there's only a glimmer of light streaming in. Someone grabs me and Indra into a crooked little corner.

My heart stops, thinking that this is it. This is the moment we get captured.

'It's us,' Faye whispers and motions for us to be quiet. Even though it's dark, we know that it is Faye and Nihal without a doubt.

The citizens continue to run through the alleyway, and we just wait there, quietly, as they swarm away.

# Chapter 13

A little while later, things finally subside, and all the zombie-like citizens are gone, scattered around elsewhere. There must have been hundreds of them that were chasing after us.

Indra scouts the area and comes back. 'The coast is clear.'

We don't say it out loud, but we all know where we're heading—the hill. It's the only place where we feel like we'll be safe. It's our own little haven.

It doesn't take us long to reach there and when we do, we are stopped by the sight in front of us. The whole area is filled with soldiers, circling and keeping watch at the bottom of the hill and around the area.

*What do we do now?* I try to silently pass a message to Indra, but he just gives me a confused look instead.

I whisper, 'What do we do now?'

'What do you think we should do?' Indra whispers back.

I really thought that when I asked the question, one of them would have an answer. Not ask the question back! It's like talking with myself in my own mind.

'I think it's best to get out of here. We'll only get caught if we stay here,' Faye says.

'But where can we go that isn't being monitored?' Nihal asks.

Faye looks at each of us. 'Where do you guys have in mind?'

We stand there in silence as we think of a temporary hideout for the night as the sun is setting. Our domiciles are definitely the number one place they'll be waiting for us so that's a complete no. Now that I think about it, Killen is a really hard place for fugitives to hide. I don't know if I should applaud that or stress out about it. In our current situation, the latter is an obvious answer.

'We could go back to the place where we came from?' Nihal suggests.

'In that dark alley?' Indra asks, and he does not look particularly happy about the idea.

'Yeah! You have a better idea than that?' Nihal gives Indra a menacing look. In certain aspects, Nihal's right. This isn't the time to be fussy, especially now that we are running for our lives.

Faye gestures for us to back away, 'There are two soldiers walking in our direction. We really need to go now!'

I suddenly become wary of Faye and stop to make sure that she is being herself and is not being possessed by someone. I scan her face to check, and she makes an expression that I am familiar with—that frown with creases lining her forehead whenever she's facing a problem that she can't solve at the Academy. We tiptoe back to the heart of the city. The citizens are scattered around everywhere. Based on the odd way they're acting right now, I don't think they are themselves again.

Some are walking around in circles, some are motionless as though they have shut down mid action, and some are just standing still.

As we get closer to the alleyway, we realize that we can't continue any further. They're in there too, pacing around the alleyway, waiting to be ordered around.

'Guys! In here!' Nihal whispers and we follow him inside a café just around the end of the block from the dark alleyway, which is getting a whole lot darker since the sun has already set.

We scatter across the café to ensure no one is around. But judging by its interiors, it looks like the place was abandoned and ravaged not too long ago. We gather back in the front, where the seating area is, and each give the all clear. There is no one around here.

Faye draws the blinds, and we all slump in partial relief since we're still not truly safe. I don't know if we'll ever be, honestly.

'I'm hungry!' Nihal announces.

'Seriously, Nihal?' Faye looks at him, perplexed by his announcement. 'We're in this situation, and all you can think about is food right now?'

'I'm a human being, too, okay? We need food to live,' he defends himself.

Faye sighs in frustration. 'Can't you starve yourself a little for the greater good of. . . everything? Especially with the situation we're currently in?'

'Who do you think I am? Someone with a saviour complex, like you?'

I sigh, *here we go again!*

She laughs. 'Me? A saviour? Well, I am really flattered. I really am!'

He gives her a pointed look. 'Who else would I be talking about? Aeni?'

'Hey! Don't involve me in your petty arguments,' I say while looking out the window for any intruders.

'You hear that, Faye? Petty arguments!' Nihal kicks a chair. 'I'm so sick of this!'

'You think we're not sick of it?' I whisper silently. I say it to myself, but they hear it too, and turn to look at me fleetingly.

'Whatever, Nihal!' Faye slumps down on a chair and sighs heavily. 'I'm done.'

'I am too, for your information.'

Nihal storms into the kitchen, looking for food. Faye watches his retreating figure and murmurs, 'Idiot!'

I don't think letting them know what they've just done is going to make the situation any better—arguing and bantering is not doing anyone any good at all. So, we just sit there in silence, away from Faye who is still looking out the window, and Nihal, who is still back in the kitchen. No doubt he's stuffing himself with food right now. How can he even have an appetite right now? I know we've been really good friends for years, but there are some things that I don't get about him.

Nihal is making an awful lot of noise for someone who just wants to fill his stomach. But moments later, he comes back with an armful of packaged pastries and dumps them on the table. We all look at him, and he smiles like nothing's happened. 'We need a plan.'

Faye snickers. 'Does the plan involve eating the whole café out because you can sign me out for that.'

He continues to smile and says calmly. 'I admit I was hangry and not being myself and for that, I am sorry, but now, I am going to be the bigger person and ignore what our sweet Faye here just said to me. What I want to talk about now is that we need a solid and concrete plan to save ourselves. To save our lives.'

*What has gotten into him?*

Faye has her back against the window. 'He's right.'

'What's the big plan you have in your mind then?' She crosses her arms and gets closer to him as if to intimidate him.

'This is probably the craziest idea I've ever had. It just came to me when I had a bite of that pastry, which I'm not even sure is good at this point but drastic times call for drastic measures. Anyway, that's beside the point.' Nihal pauses and belches as he pushes aside the opened pastry. 'I cannot guarantee that we can get out alive by executing this crazy idea of mine.'

'Ever the optimist.' Indra copies Faye's words as if to press Nihal's buttons further.

Nihal ignores him again and looks at us warily. 'I am not kidding. This could be a fatal but brilliant escape off the island and away from those zombie-like people out there.'

I guess I still look confused by his words because he places a map on top of the pile of pastries. Faye is the first one to take a closer look at the map. I, too, make my way over to them. The map looks old, as though it's been around for a long time. It also has fold marks, like the owner of the map has been bringing it everywhere they go, which would be appropriate because owning maps is forbidden in Killen.

'Where did you find this?' Faye asks.

'I found it in a can inside the cupboard.' Nihal looks smug.

'I'm guessing that whoever owns this map will want to keep it hidden there,' I say. I know I'm stating the obvious. It feels as though we just found a treasure that we never looked for in the first place. This changes everything, even though it's definitely a rocky and uncertain road ahead. But having my friends around, it feels like I can take on the impossible.

Indra's eyes widen. 'No way.'

'Yes way!' Nihal hoots but immediately tones his excitement down, when Faye glares at him.

'Are you thinking what I'm thinking?' I ask them for confirmation.

'Do you know what this means?' Indra's eyes are sparkling with delight.

'We can leave Killen.' I whisper.

# Chapter 14

'Are you crazy? You're suggesting that we leave the island and leave Killen altogether?' Faye says it all in a single breath. She looks so furious. I have never seen her as angry as this, and it is not a good thing.

Nihal understands how crazy his plan is, yet he remains calm as he tries to comfort Faye. 'There is no reason to be mad right now, Faye. I'm just trying to have a healthy discussion here. I was only trying to give a suggestion, not forcing the plan. But given our very limited choices, perhaps even none, we can't really be picky. Maybe this chance is already a godsend. A blessing in disguise. Just try to digest and imagine it first, considering we're talking about our lives being at stake here.'

'I don't think it's a bad idea, actually, when you think about it. Crazy, most likely. But it's the most sensible one we have for now. One that gives me hope for our lives.' Indra, for once, actually agrees with Nihal, who doesn't even try to hide his surprise and just smirks widely.

'Do you guys even hear yourself right now?' Faye is looking at them like she doesn't know them anymore.

Nihal frowns, 'Well do you have a better idea than that, Faye?'

She is taken aback but then says these words without a doubt: 'We could turn ourselves in.'

Nihal is about to kick a chair but stops himself short. 'This again! Is that all you bloody think about? Turning ourselves in? Don't you get it? We've done nothing wrong here! We are innocent. We have been accused of something we don't even know why, and we are being called traitors. Being accused of committing treason. And that's your best solution to the situation we're facing right now? Come on, Faye. I'm sure you can do better than that.'

'We can tell them that—'

'And then what? They'll give us a second chance? I don't know where you think we live right now, probably Fantasyland, but wake up! This is Killen! Do you really think that the Permaisuri would like to hear our testaments and our pleas as we beg for mercy? She'll send us straight to the Remote Island without a second thought, and with whatever is waiting for us there, we'll die there. Is that what you want?'

Faye walks towards the window, facing the other way and has her back to us.

Indra nudges me. 'Aeni, say something.'

I look at him. 'What do you expect me to say?'

He gives me a pointed look, and I understand what he's silently saying. I sigh and contribute to the conversation before he tries to nag me more for no reason. 'I can't say that Nihal's plan is the most brilliant idea, but I can say that it's not the worst idea ever.'

Indra sighs. 'Dude, get to your point. We do not need to hear you talk about your nonsense crap.'

'What I'm saying is that I agree with Nihal's idea.'

'Why does that not surprise me?' Faye mumbles to herself. She turns around so quickly that I think Nihal may just have flinched. 'What about our families? Are we just going to leave them here?'

'They're being controlled. They're not themselves. Even if we drag them with us, there's no guarantee that we'll be safe. They could be trying to kill us over and over or the army officers could be following our trail.'

'What makes you think this plan will work out?' Faye stands her ground.

Indra stands up and places his arms on her shoulders, looking directly in her eyes. 'We won't know that unless we try, Faye. We don't know.'

'We don't know what it's like to be out there either,' she adds.

Nihal points to the paper on the table. 'But we have a map. It could be advantageous for us.'

I pick at my fingers anxiously as my gaze flits between Nihal and Faye. The silence that follows is agonizing.

Faye clenches her jaw and sighs. 'When do we leave?' Faye asks, but she still looks wary of even the thought of running away.

I can't deny that I feel the same way. Are we really leaving Killen? What is going to happen to our families? My ma? I quickly push the thought to the back of my mind because if I continue, I might start crying.

'I'd say our best chance is to leave at dawn,' Indra suggests, walking back to his seat and, surprisingly, we all agree.

'Do you think . . .' Nihal begins but stops himself.

'Do you think what?' Indra says quietly.

'Can't we try to see our families?' Nihal pauses, trying hard not to lose it. 'You know, for the last time.'

I stare up at the ceiling, opening my eyes wide, hoping my tears won't betray me. I don't say anything, and luckily, Indra takes over, 'I'm sorry, man. I don't think that will be a good idea. We don't even know where to begin looking for them. They can be anywhere, and we have the citizens and army officers on our trail. It just won't do, I'm afraid.'

I don't think that I can keep still right now though. I can't stop thinking about the fact that we're really doing this—leaving the Central Island and our families behind. I don't think anyone has had the guts to do this. But I bet they weren't in a life and death situation either. But we are now. Besides, maybe, there are others out there who have attempted to do this, but it's unheard of.

I look around the café warily, scared that someone might pop out and find us in our newly discovered hideout. 'I'm going to explore the place,' I say to no one in particular, hoping that no one wants to tag along.

'I'm coming with you!' Indra says and we go to the kitchen in the back.

I sigh, there goes my chance. I have to get it together or he'll see there's something wrong with me. I take a few deep breaths, wipe my face with my sleeves, and hope that he won't notice.

I immediately make myself busy as I stare around the messy kitchen. The utensils are all over the place. Indra holds up a knife that has been used to slice a loaf of bread. 'Find anything useful that we can use to bring with us,' I say not looking his way.

He nods, and I head to the back of the kitchen and stumble upon a flight of spiral stairs going to an upper level. This style of stairs is very rare. I yell out, 'I'm heading upstairs.'

I go up the narrow steps and halt as I reach the second floor. It's dark and musty up here and there's barely any light coming from the window. I switch on a light bulb in the centre of the room. It illuminates the room. I scan it. There's a chest of drawers, two of which have been left open, a mattress in the middle of the room, and a sliding door leading to another room. I slide the door open and the things that greet me on the other room definitely catch my eye.

'That's definitely something we can bring with us,' Indra stares in wonder.

'What are you doing up here?' I hiss at him, startled by his presence right behind me.

'There's nothing down there that we can bring. But we can definitely bring these!' Indra points at the wall, eyes wide in shock.

On the wall opposite us, rest weapons of every kind you can imagine. Guns, swords, rifles, and even a few grenades. I stare at them in fascination and stop Indra every time he gets too close, in case one of us accidentally sets something off.

It is forbidden to own these weapons. I can't help but wonder—whoever was the owner of this café must have been really bold to have such a collection. Or could this café have served as an undercover office? Or the café owner must abide by no one's rules but their own. I admire them for their rebelliousness because I don't think I, or anyone that I know of, can ever reach their level.

'There's a room up here, a bathroom too. Great, we can lay low here for the night.' Nihal's voice comes from the other side of the room.

I turn around in surprise, too wrapped up in our new-found discovery that I didn't hear him coming up the stairs.

Footsteps can be heard coming from behind us. 'Okay, now this is just crazy!' Faye murmurs.

Indra has his eyes fixed on the wall of weapons, 'This is a sign! The universe is helping us right now! They're telling us to leave the island.'

Faye looks angry for reasons I can't comprehend. She still must not want to leave and hearing Indra is clearly making her even more furious. She grumbles, 'I truly cannot believe this!'

Nihal makes his way to us and crosses Faye on his way. He pays her no mind, and his gaze instantly lands on the weapons. 'Wow,' he says, remaining where he is and examining each of the weapons carefully.

Faye goes inside the bathroom and slams the door behind her.

The three of us look at one another and just shrug. Typical Faye. It must be taking a toll on her, breaking the rules and hoping to run from whoever it is that is trying very hard to capture us. She's always been the most rational one among us. She always plays out every possibility in her mind, only choosing the one that, most probably, has the best outcome. The rest of us, not so much.

I take a few steps back from the danger of the weapons and the two shocked faces. Obviously, we rarely get to see these kinds of things in Killen, as owning any kind of a dangerous possession is punishable under the High Law.

We really must be living in the strictest city in the world. So much so that, sometimes, I think that we don't get to live our lives the way we want to here. Killen limits us in every way, and the more I think about it, the more I despise it.

Stressing myself out more than I should is the worst thing to be doing right now.

Suddenly, it feels like the emotional turmoil I suffered today has finally caught up with me. I lean against a wall, as far as I can be from the weapons, and sit down on the cold floor. I lightly bang my head against the wall, begging for none of this to be happening. When I open my eyes, I hope I'll be back in my domicile, everyone will be back to normal, and these weird incidents will never have occurred.

But when I open my eyes, I still am where I was when I closed my eyes a moment ago. In the dark and musty room where my life literally sucks. We are running away from our homes. What other teenagers have such thoughts flooding their minds? None that I know of.

'Tired?' Faye slumps down beside me after coming out of the bathroom.

I open my eyes, 'Of everything.'

'I want your honest opinion.' Faye looks unsure.

My ears perk up, curious as to what she is about to say. 'About what?'

'Do you really think we should leave Killen?'

I think about her question and weigh the options. I still come to the same conclusion: 'What other options do we have?'

'Is that really what you think? Of course we have other options that can be considered,' Faye adds.

*Not this again!*

'Faye,' I turn my head sideways so that I can look at her, 'what do you expect me to say?'

'I just want to know what you really think.' She looks honest.

'You want to know what I think about all this?' I gesture for emphasis. 'I think that none of us deserves to be in this position. But we are in it anyway, and there's nothing we can do about it. I don't know what you're so afraid of, but we just have to man up. Or woman up? If you don't want to admit to what you're really feeling, don't worry about it because we're all scared too, even though some of us don't openly show it.'

She looks at the floor, forlorn. 'It's not that I—'

She is interrupted when the boys come into the room, looking like she is at a loss of words.

'Faye, have you seen the weapons back there?' Nihal asks, actually wanting to know her answer.

'I haven't bothered to,' Faye responds coldly.

'But seriously, though, don't you guys think that this could be a sign? What are the odds of us walking into a building that has stocked such weapons? I'd say slim to none, but we did it anyway.' He seems proud about finding this café.

I'm annoyed. Why did we have to walk into this particular building that has put these ideas into Nihal's mind? Don't even get me started on the map. That was just bad luck. It feels like we're risking our lives even more than before, but again, what other choice do we have?

The look that Faye has is one of nothing but pure anger. It's like she's a walking flame that can erupt within seconds ever since the fight back at the Academy. That was when I saw some serious changes in her.

'What do you guys think? We need a plan, though, right?' Indra sits up and looks a bit serious.

'A plan, yeah,' I respond.

He spreads the map out between us, and the three of us start to come up with plans that we desperately hope will get to see the light of day and help us survive it all. Initially, Faye remains in the sidelines but, soon enough, joins us reluctantly, only responding when necessary.

# Chapter 15

The following night, I lie on my back, staring at the low ceiling and into the space above it. I wonder about the world, the people outside and everything my mind stumbles across.

Nihal has checked the situation outside before dozing off for the night. The citizens are still walking around, controlled by an unknown source. Night fell a long time ago, but they don't look like they're shutting down to sleep anytime soon. Even though we're in a dangerous situation, I wouldn't want to be one of the citizens outside. I don't even want to imagine myself—or my ma—in their shoes. I wonder how she is right now.

My mind can't shut off, and sleep seems so far away. I toss and turn and still my eyes refuse to close.

It's a big day tomorrow. I need to rest.

I've told myself this countless times, but I'm still wide awake. Thoughts and scenarios come and go. They're like voices in my head that won't leave, begging to be heard and demanding to stay.

'Aeni?' Faye whispers. 'Are you still awake?'

'Yeah,' I whisper back.

'Can't sleep too, huh?'

'Yeah.'

She clears her throat. 'You're seriously not going to let them bring one of those weapons, are you?'

'Maybe if we are ambushed, we can be prepared, right?'

She sits up. 'Are you actually serious? We don't know anything about them, and it's very dangerous. They can accidentally shoot themselves out of shock or something.'

Faye keeps making points for me to see the opposite side of the argument, and my brain is tired from hearing the same things over and over again. She keeps convincing me and trying to make me see things in a different light.

'Faye, I get it. It's dangerous. But what will be more dangerous in a situation where we must decide to kill or be killed?' I say quietly.

She doesn't add anything more, and I take that as my cue to end the conversation. 'I'm going to sleep now.' I turn over. 'Goodnight!'

Indra snores softly beside me, and not long after, I hear Faye pulling her blanket on. Soon, I am also being transported into the land of dreams, and reality is left behind.

* * *

The next morning, around dawn, I wake up with a startle. Three sets of eyes staring at me.

'You okay there, Aeni?' Indra asks, 'Sleepy head, it's time to go. It's dawn.'

'Yeah, fine. I'm already up,' I say groggily before heading to the bathroom and closing the door quietly behind me. I open the tap and let the water rush down as I stare at myself in the mirror. I look weary and tired from the lack of sleep for the past few weeks. I'm sure I won't be able to catch up on sleep for some time now.

I take my clothes off and stand under the hot shower. I feel alive, awake, and slightly fresher than before.

Faye knocks on the door, and I yell out, 'Yes?'

'We found some clean clothes. I'll leave them outside for you.'

I spend some time under the steaming water, thinking of multiple scenarios of how today could turn out. The probability of things going downhill and ending with us getting caught is high.

*Positive thoughts. Positive thoughts. Only positive thoughts.*

I change into clean clothes, and they're different than what I usually wear. Anyway, who am I to be complaining in this situation? I should be grateful that I'm still even alive.

I step out of the bathroom and see no sign of my friends. They must be downstairs, getting ready to leave and face the nerve-racking day. No matter what comes our way, hopefully we'll be ready and brave enough to face it.

Whatever happens, I must remain optimistic.

I go down the spiral staircase and head straight to the front of the café. Indra is shoving weapons into a rucksack, and I stop him, 'What do you think you're doing? Are those all for you?'

He looks confused for a moment. 'Won't we be needing them?'

'Let me see.' I rummage around the bag and take the weapons out one by one. Two rifles, three handguns, and a handful of grenades. I look at him. 'We don't need this much. We're not going to war.'

'Isn't it better to be prepared? We don't know what we're up against,' Indra says as he packs the weapons back in the bag.

'I still don't feel comfortable being around these many weapons,' I say, watching him pack.

Indra stops. 'It's not like we're planning to do some other funny business. We're just protecting our lives here by defending ourselves, are we not?'

'You know, he has a point,' Faye says nonchalantly, and we look at her in surprise. I was not expecting those words to come out of her mouth. None of us did. Usually, she'll be all for protesting and speaking our minds, but not today.

'Why the sudden change of mind, Faye?' I ask curious to know her answer.

'If we're doing this, we gotta do this together and be prepared for whatever comes our way.' She looks determined.

After mulling it over, I resign. 'Fine. But no rifles and no grenades.' I negotiate.

Clearly Indra doesn't agree with me as he counterattacks, 'One rifle, and we need those grenades, whether you like it or not.'

'No rifles and one grenade. That's all we are taking with us.' I stand my ground and look at them. 'That goes for the rest of you. You can only take one choice of a weapon with you, but no rifles and one grenade, which Indra will bring with him, will be enough for our plan.'

'Fine!'

Indra goes back upstairs to return them where they belong. But surely, the owner wouldn't mind that we're taking some of their weapons. I just hope they won't mind, since it'll all be for the good cause of defending ourselves in this unfair and unmatched battle.

'I'll go and look around the area outside for a while. I'll be back,' I announce. They don't give me any approval, so I leave the safe confines of the building.

I walk slowly to the main street that will lead me to the City Hall and, so far, there is no sign of the citizens. The market feels quiet and lifeless as I stroll around while the sun is rising up ahead. On normal days, the road would be crowded and bustling with activity from this early hour.

'Are we good to go?' Indra walks up beside me.

I turn my head around to look at him and respond, 'Yeah.'

'Are you nervous?'

There's no point in trying to pretend to be brave when I clearly am not, 'How can I not be nervous?

We're about to do something that no one has ever done before.'

'I know.' He scans the surrounding. 'Anyway, here's your pack. We've packed some food, clothes, and other necessities in there. It could all be junk—we've just put together whatever we found lying around the café—but you never know when you might need it.'

'Thanks,' I say, and I really mean it. I would never have been able to do this all alone. I'm so glad my friends are here with me, even if we're about to go down together. It's still better than being all alone, confronting your own downfall. I don't even want to imagine it. It is a scary road to venture onto.

'Inside it, there's also a handheld gun, just in case. Maybe it can help you feel better? Only in case anything happens and the situation calls for it.'

*Why doesn't that surprise me?* I don't check the contents of the pack and sling it on my shoulders. When the time comes, I'll use it. I know I will.

'Here they come,' Indra says as Nihal and Faye step out of the café and walk towards us.

Nihal looks concerned as he quietly says, 'Are you sure we can't reconsider my suggestion from last night?'

Even though I want to let it happen with all my might, I snap out of it, 'It's too risky, I'm sorry. But I'm sure our families will be alright. It's for the best.'

I want to believe my own words, yet I'm as sceptical as the rest of them.

Faye speaks up, 'Remember that whatever happens, stick close together.'

Nihal nods looking resigned, 'Okay, then. Let's do this!'

We stand in a straight line and scan the surrounding ahead of us. We start walking step by step towards the City Hall, brimming with hopes of getting off this island and away from the danger that keeps trailing us.

# Chapter 16

As we get closer to City Hall, we are stopped by the unmatched force of the army. There are probably around a hundred army officers here, milling and pacing around. It is their job to protect Killen from any harm or danger. And right now, we are that danger, which makes us a menacing threat.

My hands start to shake in fear, and I feel my legs giving up on me just at the mere thought of having to go against them. My friends must feel the same way. Indra grabs whatever weapon he can find inside the bag. Nihal takes a step back as if wanting to run away. Faye just looks mad.

One of the army officers who sees us starts to move. I am not given the chance to further think about it as we look at one another and nod before Nihal yells out, 'Hey!'

They all look our way and immediately, the realization of who we are dawns upon them. A commander points her finger in the direction of where we are standing in the vast area of the City Hall, 'Fugitives! Traitors! Capture them!'

'Wait!' I yell out, and they momentarily stop in their tracks. I put my hand up in the air to try and pledge our innocence, 'Please! We mean no harm! We just need you to listen to us!'

The commander crosses her arms, 'Why should I do that, girl? What do you have to say for yourselves?'

'Please, just listen to us,' Nihal looks close to tears and utters in frustration.

'Fine. Speak,' the commander relents.

I start out, 'Why do you wish to capture us when we have done nothing wrong?'

'You said you wanted to speak but now you're questioning me?' the commander scoffs, 'I have no time for this.'

'Please!' Faye begs. 'We must know.'

'You are a threat to the people, and we are doing our jobs to protect the city from harm that all of you can cause.'

'But what kind of threat? Do you have any proof of what we have done to be labelled a threat to the people and the city or are you just accusing us and blaming it all on us?' Indra hollers.

'A threat is still a threat.'

'This is just nonsense!' I yell out, my insides are growing hotter as each second goes by. 'You think of us as a threat when we clearly have done nothing wrong! What kind of army officers are you? What were you even trained to do in the military and how are you qualified for your jobs? You clearly don't hold the honour of your position if this is the way you get things done. Well, let me tell you something that is the raw and honest truth. You don't deserve to be army officers. You are a disgrace to the people and the city!'

'We were given orders and—'

'From whom? The Permaisuri?' Faye asks, finally looking interested in the conversation.

'It is none of your business. We have our orders and as proud soldiers of Killen, we do not question or negotiate. We do nothing but comply with the orders that have been given to us. Failing to do so is an act that can be sentenced under the High Law. Do you still not get this?'

'Let me talk to her! Let me make my argument and plead to her as innocents because, for the last time, I will repeat: WE HAVE DONE NOTHING WRONG!' I say aloud with a clear hint of anger.

The commander laughs. 'You dare to meet her? You peasant little ones dare to meet with our great Permaisuri? The queen who rules over Killen? You must be joking.'

'Did she order you to do this?' Faye asks again, clearly relentless.

The commander looks annoyed to hear the question again, 'It doesn't matter who it came from. Orders are orders.'

At her response, Faye looks immensely surprised and tells us urgently, 'We need to go. We need to get out of here right now.'

'Hold on, Faye. We're still not done here.' Indra keeps his gaze on the commander, who is smirking and looks very proud right now.

She won't be feeling like she's won soon. In fact, she won't be able to feel at all.

'Are we done here?' she fakes a yawn. 'Armadas, get them all!'

'We need to split them up,' I whisper. 'Indra, you come with me and the rest of you guys go together. Remember to make a half round then come straight back to the City Hall.'

We all nod, and somehow, we can't stop the look that clearly shows that whatever happens, this is it. There's no turning back now.

Without another word, they storm away. I say to Indra, who is looking at their retreating backs with deep sorrow, 'Come on! We have to go.'

And we run. We will cover the left side and pass by the Academy, along the river, while Nihal and Faye will cover the right side and into the hub, into the alleyways and maze-like streets. They have got the easier route while ours is more obvious and exposed, but that's okay. We'll just have to outrun them and hope that we don't have to fight them off because then, we're obviously doomed.

We're nearing the City Hall, and I don't stop, I give it my all and run faster. The commander stands alone and unguarded on the podium. She looks angry yet calm, like she knows she's not about to lose to a bunch of teenagers.

I stop right at the edge of the podium and the soldiers stop too when their commander orders them to.

'Back again right where it all started. Aren't you a bright little one or . . . should I say not?' she chuckles to herself and orders in a commanding voice, 'Seize them!'

I don't think, I just act—Indra and I each grab the commander. I pin her down by the shoulders while Indra mutters 'sorry' and wraps his arms around her feet so she can't move. We tumble to the ground in a heap, and I don't let go. One of the soldiers takes a step forward, and I yell out, 'Step back!'

He takes another step forward, and I yell out, harder and louder, 'Step back! Stay right where you are or . . .' I hesitate, 'I'll snap her neck.'

He doesn't know that it was just an empty threat, but I try to remain formidable anyway.

The commander laughs. 'You wouldn't dare, girl.'

I whisper in her ear as if taunting her, 'Oh, you have no idea what I'm capable of.'

How long do I have to pull this off until Nihal and Faye get here? What is taking them so long? They should be here by now!

And where the hell is this courage and bravery coming from? Who am I kidding right now? Of course, I wouldn't dare harm or even think of killing her.

'Let go of me, and I will tell my men to let you go,' the commander says quietly.

'How can I believe you?' Aeni asks sceptically.

As they say, trust no one, and especially don't trust someone like the commander. She's manipulating me. Someone like her would say whatever they have to in order to just get the upper hand, and I am not falling for it.

Indra shakes his head. He seems to be struggling to maintain his hold on her. Even if it's two against one, they don't stand a chance. He mouths, 'Don't.'

'I am a woman who sticks to her words.'

*I will not yield.*

'That doesn't convince me. Don't think for a second that I'm someone who is easy to manipulate. You have clearly underestimated me.'

The commander laughs maniacally and seems as though she can't stop. My thoughts wander to the possibility of her actually going mental. Seriously, where are Faye and Nihal? I can't stall them for too long.

No, it can't be. They must be alright and will be here soon. No, it's impossible.

I want to slap myself for having these thoughts of what ifs.

They'll be here. I just know that they'll be.

My anxiety must be obvious because the commander smirks and says, 'Your friends couldn't make it, huh?'

She is really getting on my nerves now. I swing my leg and sit on top of her. With my saliva splattering around, I yell, 'Shut up!'

'Why? Because I'm stating the truth? Or are you too afraid to listen to the truth? But seriously, what is it you're trying to do here? You're just stalling everyone because, sooner or later, you and your pathetic friends will go down.'

I stare her down. 'You're wrong and I'm going to prove it. You and your men are the ones who are going down.'

'Aeni! Look!' Indra exclaims excitedly as we see two figures running in our direction.

I sigh in relief, they made it after all. Now it's my turn to smirk. 'What did I tell you? And now, you're going down.'

Army officers trail behind Faye and Nihal, who are showing no sign of stopping or slowing down—determined to capture them. They pass the other group of army officers that is tailing us and, as it was driven by a force, all of them come running towards us.

I dread for the next step in our plan. I would never have dreamed of taking it this far, but now, it is us or them. And I choose us.

'Now!'

Indra looks away, eyes barely open in fear, as he pulls the trigger for the grenade and throws it towards the army officers that are flocking in our direction. I shove the commander hard towards her men and run as far away as we can and take cover by cowering into a crouch as there's not a lot of time before the grenade explodes.

The impact of the explosion causes ringing in my ears. It sends guilt and shivers coursing throughout my body. I can't believe we did that. We killed all those people for our own survival.

It was the only way.

I cough as I open my eyes and scan the area to witness the aftermath of our plan. I see smoke, ashes, and fire. I quickly glance away before I get a glimpse of the bodies lying around lifeless—no longer among the living.

I look up and scan the surrounding. My eyes land on a sight that makes me catch my breath.

*Ma!*

I want to call her but someone blocks my view. 'Come on, Aeni! We need to go!' Indra pulls me up and I push him away. When I look at the spot where I just saw Ma, she is nowhere to be found anymore. Did I just conjure her up in my mind or was it really her?

I don't have time to dwell on this as Indra yanks me away. He leads the way, as he's the one in charge of the map. We go into the City Hall and down a flight of stairs until I see a train. It looks different than the trams I have been riding all my life. It has to be different, since this one runs underwater and will take us to our chosen destination of the other islands in Killen.

The doors open automatically and we slink inside. We follow Nihal as he walks straight to the front of the car and into the control room. It's pretty straightforward, since everything can be done with the clicks of a few buttons.

There are only five buttons in total—Central, Linggi, Boundary, Remote, and the last one is Mahkota.

I don't think twice as I press the last button with the destination of the royal palace.

The train immediately embarks on the journey and we leave the island behind.

'Uh, Aeni? Which button did you just press?' Indra is the first to raise concern.

Nihal adds, his eyes wide, 'Why are we heading there?'

'To seek redemption and answers.' I take a seat and watch as the island we have lived on all our lives moves far away as the train moves further into the water, headed to its coursed destination.

# PART III

# Chapter 17

The doors slide open and we hesitantly look out the station to scan the area outside of the train, anticipating whatever might be lurking around out there. Faye is the first one to brave stepping outside. She scans the area and nods at us. We follow her into unfamiliar territory.

Faye slows down, and she nudges us to tell us someone's coming. It's the royal army officers. The difference between them and the regular army officers are their uniforms. While the regular army officers are in black, the royal army officers are in bright red.

Faye steps into the light to lure the two army officers who are chattering away.

'Hey! What are you doing here?' they demand.

She shrugs and the army officers march towards her. Before they can reach her, the boys ambush them from the sides, hit their heads with their packs, and they collapse in a heap on the floor.

'Nice one!' Nihal high five's with Indra. They look proud of themselves and I try to warn them, 'There's more coming. Don't act so proud yet.'

I know what you're thinking. I'm such a party pooper.

We continue into the maze to find our way out of the station and see no sign of another royal army officer yet.

'Shouldn't we just get caught to beg for mercy from the Permaisuri?' Indra suggests.

I don't reply, not knowing how to respond to the question.

'Do you expect us to sneak into the palace unnoticed when the palace is the most secure building in Killen?' Nihal asks in horror. 'Everyone knows that is impossible.'

I sigh. 'Okay, let's think about it rationally. If we ambush our way in, the probability of us not getting caught is higher than us surrendering ourselves.'

'Hold on a minute, that wasn't part of the plan!' Nihal screeches.

'We need to improvise. We don't have much of a choice.'

'Yeah, and we need to get out of this station first,' Faye murmurs.

'Look!' Indra exclaims.

We turn to look at him and he points to what is waiting before us. Row after row of the royal army officers are standing there, and they're smirking at their new-found prey.

'Well, well, well! Would you look at these little ducklings! Are you lost?' a commander of the royal army snickers. He looks sterner and more intimidating than the last commander we defeated back on Central Island.

'We are lost,' Faye says in a clear voice, indicating that she's not backing down. Not anytime soon.

'Well there, sweet chick, would you like me to show you the way then?' he smirks.

If looks could kill, he'd already be dead from the ones we were throwing his way.

'I'd rather die,' Faye says with contempt.

'What about you, shorty?' he turns his attention to a new prey—me. I look at him, absolutely disgusted.

'Hey, how about you leave them alone?' Indra yells out.

'Well, how about you mind your own freaking business?' the commander is caressing his gun in the holster of his belt.

'It is my business if it involves my friends!' Indra spits out.

'Brave boy, foolish boy,' the commander singsongs.

He looks at each one of us and condescendingly commands his army officers, 'Capture them. Dead or alive.'

He walks away, and we are met with a pack of army officers, waiting for us like wolves.

Everyone is alarmed by the enemies we must face, but Nihal is the first to react, 'What do we do now? One to one battle? Shoot them? Talk to them?' his voice trembles.

It's just one obstacle after another. I try to think or come up with a plan but seeing the daunting faces of the army officers is making it seem impossible. Again, how are we, a bunch of teenagers with no combat skill, going to go up against a group of trained army officers?

I try to let my fears go, but it's proving to be a futile exercise. I try to push it aside anyway and do my best to sound logical, 'The last one is a terrible idea.' I think some more. 'There's around ten of them. So, we have to split them up equally—you and Indra take six and Faye and I will take two each?'

Indra looks sceptical about my suggestion. 'Ten against four—are you sure you both can manage two each?'

I try to appear brave even though I'm cowering on the inside. 'I don't know.'

'How about we go seven and three?' Indra suggests.

Nihal looks horrified, 'Seven? Who do you think I am? A superhero? How is that even equal?'

'We are left with no choice here! It's either that or surrender!' I yell too loudly.

The commander tsks, 'How much longer are you going to take to decide? You know what? Take your time, we have all day long.' His voice is laced with sarcasm.

I ignore him. Nihal and Indra scowl at him.

Faye just looks annoyed and she responds to Nihal, 'Do you think that just because we're girls, we can't beat down a bunch of army officers? We're living in the thirty-first century, for god's sake! Enough of this thing about women not being able to fight like men! We'll split them evenly.'

Nihal looks ashamed and I give him a look that says *what?* as I give in to Faye's suggestion, 'Fine, then we'll split them evenly.'

Faye sighs. 'That's okay. But don't ever underestimate us again.'

I nod and she continues, 'Don't you think now is a good time to surrender? What's the point of talking about a game plan when we know we won't make it out alive?'

'The army officers are advancing on us as we speak, and we're just delaying the inevitable by arguing like this.' I already feel defeated as I say those words.

The commander snickers, 'Are you done strategizing, or can we finally get this done and over with?'

No one bothers to reply to him. We each look at one another resolutely as if trying to find some comfort. It's almost like each of us is saying goodbye and accepting what our fates await. I have gone from going to the Academy every day, hanging out with my friends, and spending time with Ma to arriving at death's door more times than she ever has. If this is how the end of my life is going to be, I hope I don't have any regrets.

'Then what are we waiting for?' Nihal takes a step forward and gets ready for battle. 'Charge!'

At that, the army officers don't hesitate and run towards us with full force. And so do we at them.

I grab the first army officer, and I don't hesitate to do him some damage. It's better for him to get hit than the other way around. The easiest and the most effective way to attack them is to target the groin. I wish I was feeling sorry, but right now, I can only be a merciless person.

Nihal is already engaged with an army and is punching him while yelling senselessly, 'This is fun!'

I assume the fun only lasted awhile, as he gets beaten up in return. The rest of our losing squad are already yanking and pulling the army officers to the ground. For a minute, Faye is clinging on to one of the army officer's back and choking him. The man soon slumps on the floor among his other teammates.

For a while, I am struck with the feeling of hope that we're going to make it. But it seems to be wishful thinking because another troop of army officers is now arriving to knock us down and capture us—dead or alive.

*We're absolutely done for now.* What we just did—that was pure luck and determination with a hint of the full force of our energy, but I don't think we can take it anymore. I feel the pain in my ribs from one of them kicking my torso, and I am already feeling pain all over my body. Indra has blood running down his face while a few bruises are already forming. Faye is clutching her arm, her face contorted with pain. I really hope that it's not broken. Nihal is limping as he walks towards an army officer who is advancing on him. He's clearly getting tired as he fails to dodge the blow for the umpteenth time and crashes down to the ground.

'Please!' Faye begs in a slow voice as the army officer kneels down to look at her.

I put my pain away and kick him in the head. He immediately faints and hits the floor.

'Is it time to surrender now?' Nihal asks.

I'm breathing heavily as I answer, 'I think that might be our only choice now.'

I look at them for confirmation, and they all nod. This is it. This is what we've all come to—what we have achieved so far. We hope that our efforts will not be fruitless and hope that the Permaisuri will give us a bit of her time to listen to our pleas. I won't hope too much about it though. I don't know why but I have a feeling that she'll command her army to ship us straight to the Remote Island.

I raise my hands in the air as a sign of surrender and the group of army officers halt momentarily. They watch us suspiciously to gauge our motives as most of us are limping, leaning on the wall for support, and even lying on the ground. They double check to make sure we have pulled out a white flag before they finally put their weapons down.

One of them takes a few steps forward and announces, 'You will be arrested for breaking the High Law of trespassing and attempting treason against the country. It is my duty to—'

A grenade is thrown from behind us to the centre of where the army is standing, and a moment later, I hear a voice yell, 'Watch out!'

We don't hesitate and run away from it. Indra has to half carry Nihal with him. We only get a little further away before it explodes. My eyes are stinging, and I hear my friends coughing beside me. Amid the smoke, a figure is walking towards us and stops just short of us, 'Are you okay?'

Is this a dream? Am I dead?

As my senses turn back to normal, and I take a real look at the figure, I'm surprised to find a girl my age.

# Chapter 18

'Are you okay?' the girl yells out. She waves her hand in front of my face.

She appears slightly concerned as she scans my face, making sure I am not seriously injured. The boys keep looking at her and trying to uncover the mysterious identity of the girl who just came out of nowhere to rescue us. She seems uncomfortable about their gazes and crouches down to collect a discarded gun. She checks to make sure there are still bullets inside and cocks her head at our antics, 'Hope that didn't scare you. You looked like you were having trouble with those guys there so I thought I'd help out. A thank you would suffice.'

Everyone finally snaps out of it and tries to stand up while clutching at their wounds. Indra helps Nihal, who needs the assistance.

I'm the first one to speak up, 'Thank you for rescuing us. We might have been dead by now if you didn't come to our rescue.'

She scrutinizes the gun. 'You're welcome.'

One of the royal guards is starting to stir and Indra hisses, 'I think we need to go now. We need to get out of here!'

'Can you walk?' I ask Faye, and she nods while walking to the end of the corridor, where the boys already are.

My friends turn to leave. I stop before I turn to follow them out of this place. I ask the girl, 'Aren't you coming too?'

'I'm not,' her reply is short.

'Do you know the way out of here?'

She nods and I give her a look of someone who is both desperate and hopeless without meaning to.

I plead, 'Could you tell me?'

The frown is still plastered on her face, and I am really starting to get impatient here.

'Aeni?' Indra yells out from a distance, sounding impatient. 'Are you coming?'

I ignore him and ask the girl, my tone not exactly friendly and cheery, 'As you can probably tell, we're sort of in a hurry here.'

'Yes, I can see that,' she gives me a pointed look. 'But as you can probably tell from the vibe I'm giving off, maybe I don't want to tell you the directions.'

'Excuse me?'

*This is absurd*, I think to myself.

'Oh, you are serious?' I ask bewildered by the arrogant girl. You know how people say that first impressions matter? I would like to argue with whoever said those idiotic words because people can be just as impossible even after their first impressions have been made.

Never judge a book by its cover, am I right?

'Look, I don't know what your problem is exactly but could you help us out a bit here? Can't you for once do a kind deed for the sake of humanity?' I plead. I really want to get out of here and would very much like to see another day, alive. I don't add that since I'll pretty much be looking for trouble and nothing other than embarrassment.

'Kind deed? Are you actually talking about kind deeds? You have no idea . . .' she mumbles to herself and looks at the floor as if thinking about what I just said.

She finally looks up and says, 'Fine! I'll help you.'

*Wow, I can't believe that actually worked! I'm coming for you, hope!*

She walks confidently to my friends and leads the way, 'Follow me!'

She directs us around the station, which should be called a maze and not a station. She doesn't even stop to think twice as she turns into one corridor after another.

'Can we trust her?' Nihal whispers.

I shrug, unsure about it myself. 'I guess only time will tell.'

Faye shakes her head, 'I don't have a good feeling about this. She doesn't look like the type to help out others just like that.'

'That's what I think too!' Indra agrees a little too loudly.

I take a sneaky glance at the girl. She's acting like nothing happened and doesn't look like she heard anything from our conversation. Could she be pretending not to hear anything or is she just not interested at all? This girl is very hard to crack and figure out.

'But if anything happens, just be prepared. She could be working for Permaisuri,' Faye whispers, looking at her with suspicion.

She turns around, making a 360-degree turn. The look on her face is enough to even make the royal army officers not to think twice before scattering off. She storms towards me and grabs my shirt. 'You can say things about me, but you will not say any nonsense about me that is associated with that woman because the one thing I will never ever do is work for her! I would rather die than to work under her. If you even mention her name again, I will leave you here to rot away!'

We are left speechless. Indra's mouth is hanging open, surprised by the outburst, and I can't say that I'm anything different. My heart is beating so hard that I feel like it might be leaping out of my chest.

She turns around and continues on her way, her stride even bigger and faster than before.

'What just happened?' Indra whispers.

No one replies and, solemnly, we follow the girl. Hopefully, she will still lead us out of this station because I'm getting so sick of this place.

I match her stride and start walking beside her. 'We are really sorry for what we just said behind your back. We promise that it won't happen again. Ever.' I pause before continuing in a tiny voice, 'Please don't turn us in?'

She stops and looks at me, 'Why would I do that?'

I momentarily glance at the new girl and ask her, 'You were the one who threw the grenade, right?'

She scrutinizes me and nods. The frown doesn't leave her face. She doesn't bother replying as she looks at the ceiling and murmurs to herself, 'This must be it.'

She looks at Indra, who appears the least injured out of everyone. 'Could you give me a lift?'

'Uh . . . oh, yeah sure!'

He lifts her up, and she disappears wherever she just went out of the hole. A moment later, she lets her head down, 'What are you doing? Come on up!'

'I'll go first just to make sure,' I say, 'Indra, lift me up.'

'Yeah, sure!'

He lifts me up, and I easily go through. I scan the place, and the first thing I feel is the sun streaming through the window and I feel giddy about it. *We made it out!* I take a closer look around the place—it almost looks like a home. There are papers strewn around, pillows on the floor with blankets and some stuff that must belong to the girl. I must say, the place seems really cozy.

'Aeni?' Indra whispers from down below.

'Yeah, it's cool. Come on up.' I lie down by the hole on the wood floor, 'Let's get Faye up first.'

After I've pulled her up with a lot of force, since she can only manage half of hers, Nihal is next, and finally it's Indra's turn.

'We're safe here. No one tailed us,' the girl says.

I ask for confirmation, 'Are we really outside?'

'Yes, you are. There are tunnels throughout the island, and you can easily go about from below. But only if you know how to make your way around.'

'So, you have basically memorized the tunnels?' Faye asks incredulous.

The girl nods like it's the most regular thing to do and shrugs like it's nothing new. She turns to look at me, 'So, are you guys runaways or something?'

Our lips are sealed to not give us away, but then I speak up, 'Maybe we are.'

'And, who are you?' Faye scrutinizes her.

'No one,' she's avoiding our gazes and looks at the floor. 'Just an outcast.'

I ask, 'Then why should we trust you?'

'Who said anything about trust?' She scowls. 'Look, my job here is done. You asked—no, begged—me to get you out of the maze, and I did. So, it's all up to you now and that is to leave.'

We are taken aback. Clearly, we haven't thought this through. We've made it to the Mahkota Island, but we still have so many other things to consider. What are we even expecting? The sun is going to set soon, and we have no shelter for the night even though some of us are injured. There is a big possibility that Faye's arm is broken, and she needs to get it treated as soon as possible.

'Are you telling us to leave?' I ask.

'Shouldn't you be on your way, anyway?' The girl turns to leave the room.

'Some of us are injured. Our friend here,' I point in Faye's direction, 'her arm is probably broken.'

The girl turns to look at Faye. 'Do I look like a doctor to you? A nurse? Or maybe someone who has an experience working at the infirmary?' She tsks at the expressions on our faces, which are startled by her sudden outburst. 'Guess not then.'

I refuse to give up, 'Perhaps do you know someone who can help us?'

She laughs, 'Are you kidding me right now? What makes you think I want to help you more than I should? Listen here, you probably think that I'm nice enough to help you on your way. Well, that's where you're wrong. I'm not someone who you can even consider nice. Perhaps you are too naïve about the world we live in. There is no such thing as nice people, only ones who must do whatever it takes to keep on living.'

'Who are you?' I frown. 'Are you a runaway too? Perhaps a fugitive? Like us?'

The thought catches me by surprise, and I feel a glimmer of hope spread through me. Could it be possible? That we are not the only fugitives out there and a survivor is right here in front of us. What are the odds?

She sighs. 'Probably.'

'Then you'd understand the situation we are currently in.'

'There is nothing I can do to help you. Don't you get that?' She looks resigned by my constant coercion.

'Wait.' Faye scrutinizes the girl and asks the question she just asked a moment ago, 'Who are you?'

'That is none of your business,' the girl snaps.

'Why do I have a feeling that you look so familiar to someone we all know,' Faye continues relentless. 'Have you lived in Killen before? I swear I have seen you around before.'

'I've never left this island!' the girl clarifies.

'Are you sure?' Faye persists.

She looks at Faye in complete bewilderment, 'Of course, I'm sure.'

Nihal interrogates her next. 'But you live here? In this shack? Without the Permaisuri's knowledge? It doesn't make sense.'

'I will have you know that she isn't as observant as you might think she is. She can be very ignorant sometimes.' She rolls her eyes at the mention of the person she probably hates most in the whole of Killen.

'So, who are you to her that she remains to be ignorant to you?' Faye asks.

She wants to avoid the question, but I can see that she immediately changes her mind, 'No one. Just someone who wants to be invisible.'

'Are you her maid? Is that why you live here?' Nihal looks surprised and proud of his guess. 'And is that the reason why you never left the island? It all makes sense now, why you live here. Wait, so, do all the maids have their own shacks all over the island? Who would've thought the Permaisuri could be this generous? Or perhaps she just doesn't want peasants to live under the same roof as her? Now it all makes sense and all the pieces match.'

The girl looks taken aback by all his remarks. 'No, I'm not her maid. I just . . . live and, well . . . work in the palace. I've met some of the maids too. That's all I'd say.'

'Is that true?' Faye asks, still looking doubtful.

'Yes, that's true,' the girl nods, repeatedly. 'Although only a handful of maids have their own places.' Even she's having a hard time trying to convince herself with that answer.

'I did not see that coming. So, do the military officers have their own places, too, around the island? Or is it just the maids?' Nihal can't help asking.

'I don't know about that,' she sighs. 'Enough with the questions.'

She leaves the room and comes back again a moment later with a white box. 'This is an aid kit.'

The girl seems to be holding back. I can sense that she wants to help but deep inside her, she's telling herself to not get too attached and involved in our situation. Us coming here is probably the most exciting event to have happened in her life, just like it is exciting for us that we are still alive. I'm probably reading too much into it because who do I think I am? A teller, a mind reader, or someone who can understand people?

'I'm heading off for a bit. Do whatever you want,' the girl says as she grabs a bedazzled purple backpack off the floor beside me.

I ask before she opens the front door, 'Can we at least know your name?' She looks ready to leave, but I stop her. 'My name is Aeni, that's Indra, the other girl is Faye, and Nihal is the one who kept asking you so many questions. Sorry about that.'

She looks at each one of us, thinking and processing our names before she finally says, 'My name is Laya.'

# Chapter 19

'So, does that mean she'll let us stay?' Indra is the first to break the silence after Laya leaves.

I like her name. It suits her personality. But she can obviously be nicer is all. We are, after all, four clueless teenagers who are looking for answers in this impossible maze.

'What other options do we have? Of course, we'll stay for the night. We must grab every opportunity that comes our way because how often does it happen, right?' Nihal suggests as he winces because of his injury.

'She still seems familiar to me,' Faye digs into her mind to try and figure where she's seen Laya before.

'I still have a bad feeling about this—staying here, thinking that we're safe when we have no idea what is going on outside,' I add.

'Dude, then are you suggesting we leave? How does that help at all?' Nihal asks perplexed, his mind already set on staying here for the night.

*How do I even answer him? I don't have the answers to everything!*

'How about you guys treat me first? How about that? Just give me a painkiller or something. I feel like I'm on the brink of death!' Faye is sweating profusely and clutching my thigh to manage her pain.

'All right! All right!' I yelp as she clutches me harder.

We do our best to repair the damage, but there's nothing much we can do. We don't have any experience working at the infirmary, and our resources are limited too. The aid kit only has basic necessities, and we are in a more urgent situation than what that small box can offer solutions to.

We wrap Faye's arm in bandages, forming a makeshift cast. Of course, it probably does little to nothing to help, but it is the best we can do for now to ease her pain and for her arm to recover. She has taken a few painkillers and now looks drowsy from the effect of the medicine. I grab a pillow and place it on the ground before I make her lie down. She dozes off not long after that, clearly feeling the weariness of today's events and effects of the medicine.

When I try to stand up, I shriek as the pain from my ribs shoots through me.

Indra looks at me and asks, 'Are you okay?'

I nod. 'I'm fine.'

He walks towards me and doesn't let me stand up. 'You stay there. Let me see what I can do.'

He shuffles around the contents of the box and takes out yet another roll of bandage. 'This is all we have.'

'Really, it's fine,' I assure him, but he shoots me a look that is the total opposite of assured.

'Stop bluffing around. You are not fine. Stop acting like such a hero, Aeni.'

'But don't you like it when I act that way?' I tease.

He slaps my upper arm. 'No, I don't.'

We laugh for a bit. It feels nice to laugh for a moment like this, to not worry about anything, to just let go. It helps to release some of the sorrow that I'm feeling.

'I am so tired!' Nihal announces out of nowhere. He grabs a pillow and sets it down beside Faye, who looks peaceful in her sleep. He turns around so that he is facing Faye, closes his eyes and joins her in a fitful sleep.

Suddenly, Indra turns towards me. He gives me a once over and judging from the way he's wincing, I can only guess how bad my injuries must look.

'What do you think you are doing, young lady?' Indra pretends to scold me and puts on an angry face. 'Take off your clothes right now.'

'What? Hell no! No way!'

'I'm just trying to mend your wound. Nothing more. Isn't that what friends are for?'

I still protest. 'I'll treat it myself. You can go.'

Indra relents. 'I'll leave.' He plops a bottle of ointment on the side table. 'Apply this. Call me if you need any help.'

He walks out of the room, and I take off my top. I gasp as I see the bruises that are forming across my torso. 'Ouch.'

I pop the bottle open and start lightly smearing the ointment. I wince in pain when I make contact with my bruises. But once its effect sets in, it soothes the pain. I do feel slightly better. The pain is more manageable now.

Some time passes and someone knocks the door.

I fumble with my T-shirt. 'Hold on a second.'

I put it on, making sure I'm modest now and yell, 'You can come in now.'

Indra walks in and tries to inspect me. 'How do you feel? Is it better?'

I nod and, in return, inspect his face. The blood spread across his face has now dried. I wipe it away and apply a Band-Aid on his forehead.

He touches it slightly and says, 'Thanks.'

I give him a small smile.

'Do you want something to eat?' he asks.

'Probably not. I'm tired. Feel like catching up on some sleep,' I respond.

He looks a bit disappointed. 'Oh, okay! I'll just be in the bathroom. Be right back.'

I shake my head wondering why he didn't go before.

I grab a pillow and lay down facing the wall. A moment later, he comes back into the room. He sits down and sighs before murmuring, 'My body is killing me.'

I don't have the energy to muster a response, and he's saying what we are all feeling. My eyes start to get heavier and sleep swallows me whole.

* * *

I wake up to the sound of an object crashing down to the ground. Did the army officers ambush us? I immediately sit up to scan the room for an intruder, and I find a lone figure clutching a framed picture, which is shattered. The glass has broken into a thousand pieces on the floor. So that's what fell.

'Laya?' I say quietly, not wanting to surprise her.

She scrapes the shattered glass scattered across the floor and sniffles. 'Yeah, it's just me. Sorry to wake you up. It was just a small accident.'

I help her cautiously pick and clean up the glass on the floor, not wanting to hurt myself more than I already have. She dismisses me. 'I can do it. Don't worry about it. Just go back to sleep.'

'It's fine,' I assure her. 'Besides, I don't feel sleepy anymore. I've had more than enough sleep to keep me awake for a whole day.'

She continues picking up each of the shattered glasses one by one and doesn't look at me, 'If you say so.'

After we are sure that we haven't left any glass lying around on the floor, I follow her to the kitchen and throw it away.

She rinses her hands in the sink. 'Thanks for the help.'

I bow. 'It's my pleasure! Considering you didn't kick us out, it's the least I can do.'

For the first time, under the moonlight, she smiles. I keep my calm and stay peaceful. But how can I? I didn't know that she's even capable of smiling! Let alone at a stranger who is intruding in her space! She isn't as bad as she seems after all. Maybe it's all just a façade to keep people at bay.

I return her smile, and she quickly frowns as soon as she realizes what she has done.

'Are you heading off to bed now?' I ask, just to get the conversation going. What did you expect me to ask her? The weather?

'No. I'm not that tired. And I'm sure you aren't too.'

I nod before asking, 'Oh, can I get a glass of water?'

'Knock yourself out.' She sits down on the chair and rests her cheek on her hand, facing the window outside as the trees sway in the breeze.

I sit across from her, quietly sipping my drink. I want to get the conversation going again but I don't know what to ask her. She doesn't seem like the type to pour her heart out to a complete stranger anyway. She seems closed off to me—someone who just wants to get far away from here.

'What's your story, Aeni? Why are you here? And why are you a runaway?' She grins. 'I haven't had a company in ages and I'd love to hear your story.'

I beam. 'Is the palace that boring that none of the other maids' stories interest you anymore?'

She looks confused. 'What?'

'Don't you work in the palace?' When she still looks confused, I add, not giving her a chance to get a word in, 'So, nothing interests you anymore?'

'When you've been in the palace for too long and there's no one there who you can really talk to, everything becomes dull. Everyday there feels like a rainy day when the world is a rainbow.'

She shies away as soon as she says that. I quickly tell her my story in fear that she will lose interest in me too.

She neither interrupts me nor stops me as I tell her my story and how I happened to come here.

'So, that's why you came here?' she asks when I conclude.

I nod. Suddenly, I have the urge to make her understand me. 'What do you think? Do you think us coming here was a good idea?'

'I can't say that it was bad, but I can say that you guys were certainly brave,' she says and whispers something to herself.

I lean closer to her, not having caught what she said. 'Sorry, did you say something?'

She shakes her head. 'No, I didn't. But what made you come here to this island when there are other islands to run away to? Why did you pick this specific island to head off to when it is also the most dangerous one?'

'The idea sounds more stupid than it is,' I respond. 'We're here to meet with the Permaisuri.'

She leans back as far away from me as possible, as though she wants nothing to do with me. 'Excuse me?'

I repeat, 'We're here to meet with Seri Paduka Baginda, Mahsuri, Permaisuri of Killen. As I said before, I know the idea may seem foolish when you listen to it, but it actually makes a lot of sense. We want her to hear our pleas and, hopefully, she'll let us go free.'

'You have met her before, right?' Laya asks.

'Yes, we have, of course. She comes around every three months for her usual speech at the City Hall.'

Laya eyes me as though I am, once again, a stranger to her. 'Then you know how ruthless she can be. How evil she is despite what is truly right and wrong. And do you also know that there is a specific island for lawbreakers who are sent there to whatever creatures that stay on the island? Are you aware of all this?'

'Yes . . . I am?' I say, hesitantly.

'Then what makes you think she'll ever listen to you?'

'Worth a shot. You never know unless you try?' I say again, hesitantly.

'Are you stupid or are you crazy?' She laughs, 'If I were you, I would have left Killen when I had the chance. You boarded the train and you chose this island as your destination? You couldn't have just pressed the button for the boundary and made your way out of Killen?'

'What would be the point of running away?' My comeback is weak. Yes, I am well aware of that.

'The point? Who cares what the point is? The main point is that you live the rest of your lives ahead of you. All of you live!'

'No, people who run away selfishly are cowards. They are nothing but cowards!'

'Pretending to act all mighty and brave will get you killed. Believe me.' Laya stands up and storms out of the house, not even caring that my friends are sleeping or the fact that someone outside might hear us.

# Chapter 20

I sit on the chair for a while, processing all that Laya has said to me. It was more like getting yelled at by her and it was not the best thing to be experiencing this late at night. Especially after a long and tiring day. I get that what we're doing right now—us being here—is a mistake. But so what? Everyone makes mistakes! We're not saints. We are mere human beings.

The more I think about it, the more annoyed and resentful I feel.

I stand up and head straight to my makeshift bed, which consists of a pillow and the wooden floor. I toss and turn until dawn arrives and sunlight is flooding the entire place. Why can't night-time be much longer? Then, I'd have more time to think about everything and hopefully sort out this mess.

I just wish that I'd wake up in my bed back home on Central Island and everything would go back to being normal again. I wish I was never aboard the train that lead us here.

Even though the sun has risen, and it is time to go on our way in search for our freedom, my eyes are failing as they continue to shut on their own, and I soon fall asleep.

* * *

It only felt like I was asleep for a second when I wake up with a startle. I don't know what I was dreaming about but it felt real when I yell out, 'Leave me alone!'

I sit up and stare at my surroundings. I am in the shack on the Mahkota Island, and we would like to have a little chat with the Permaisuri. Sounds wonderful, doesn't it?

'Are you awake now?' Indra asks, munching on the food from our supplies.

'What happened? What's going on?' My head has been spinning since I sat up so suddenly because I was startled.

'Nothing! We're just eating because we're hungry,' Nihal says as he puts down the now empty tin on the floor. 'You should eat something too. Or you'll starve yourself.'

'Yeah, I probably should.'

Nihal grabs my rucksack and hands it to me, his expression solemn, 'Here.'

'Thanks,' I say.

I open up a tin and get right into it. I didn't feel hungry before but now I do. I finish mine within minutes, since I eat it so heartily. Even my friends don't dare try to disturb me as I am finishing up my meal.

'That was really good!' I exclaim.

Nihal shrugs, 'Sure.'

Indra adds, 'It was fine.'

'It was okay.' Faye stares into the distance.

My friends' responses are a bit grim but I continue ignoring them. It was really good food and the least I can do is be positive about it. This is my way of trying to make myself feel upbeat when everything around me is failing miserably.

'Aeni, we need to talk about what we're going to do next. Do you have a plan?' Faye asks as she strokes her bandaged arm.

'I don't have one yet,' I reply, 'but what about you guys? Do you guys have one? After all, I can't be the only one to decide things between us. This concerns all of us, and we need to plan it all out and stick together no matter what happens. What do you say?'

'Now you're in deep trouble.'

None of my friends say this. It is Laya, who is standing in the doorway.

'Lady, I don't know why you're so against us when we have done absolutely nothing wrong to you,' Nihal says, looking annoyed.

'You're right, you haven't done anything wrong to me, it was just the words your friend here uttered that have pissed the hell out of me,' she points at me and smirks.

I am about to defend myself when Nihal speaks up, 'You don't know anything about us! What we went through and the things we've seen. You have no idea! You also have no say in what we do and how we are going to do things around here!'

'Are you done?' The smirk doesn't leave her face and it is cynical, disturbing, and effortlessly offending us all.

'No,' I look at her and it's my turn to smirk now. 'Why do you hate the Permaisuri so much? What has she done to you that has made you resent her so much, to the point that even the people around you cannot even mention her name?'

She turns her head sideways, 'That is none of your concern. You practically barged in here and made this place as if it was your own, which I do not mind. At all. But you have the audacity to ask about me and that woman? Do you have a death wish? Would you like me to grant it for you?'

She takes a step forward, and Indra stands up, trying to make himself a human shield for us all. 'Do not take a step forward.'

She takes a few steps backward, looks a little to the side and murmurs to herself, a stricken look crossing her face. 'What have I done? Who am I turning into?'

'That's right, lady! You would never win against us. It's four versus one and I think we can all tell who will win this fight!' Nihal brags, and I so desperately want to smack him right in his face.

'We are extremely sorry for intruding into your life. If we could turn back time, we wouldn't even be here in the first place but we are here and we can't turn back the time. It would be impossible. We truly apologize for all the inconveniences we have caused. We will leave now,' I say.

'Wait!' She stops us but doesn't seem to know where to steer the conversation and how she wants to say her piece.

I wait eagerly to see what she has to say, hoping that deep down she's not as evil as she seems to be.

'Should we just go or . . .' Indra suggests. I look at everyone and they all seem to agree with getting out of this shack. Now.

Nihal struggles to stand up, and Indra comes to his aid. Even Faye is retrieving her stuff that is out of her rucksack while I'm just standing there, waiting. Laya still seems to be contemplating as if she has contradicting voices telling her what to do.

'Aeni! Let's just go,' Faye pulls me out of my reverie. I look at her and she has a pleading look on her face.

I say, 'Of course. Yeah, we should go.'

We are ready to go, each of our rucksacks are on our respective shoulders except for Indra, who is holding on to both his and Nihal's rucksacks. We walk past Laya, and my hand grabs the doorknob when she yells out again, 'Wait!'

I turn around to look at Laya, who walks over to us. Beside me, Faye mumbles coherently to herself, 'What now?'

'It's not safe for you to go out there at this time,' Laya warns. Faye is ready to protest when she continues, 'Around this time, the army officers are marching around the island and if you step out of this shack, one of them will definitely see and catch you. It's a daily protocol thing to ensure maximum security on the island. But now that word has spread about you having managed to breach the island, I have no doubt that the security will be increased twofold.'

'Aeni! What do we do now?' Indra whispers but, clearly, in this small shack, his voice has travelled to Laya and she has heard what he just said.

'Wait it out and go later in the evening or go into the tunnels, which is a bad idea, since you'll definitely get lost inside them. Both of the options are not great for you, since they will lead to you getting caught, eventually. It is just a matter of how far you can go before they catch you.'

'Okay, we get it!' Faye sighs, 'So, what's your point?'

Laya looks at Faye dubiously. 'I think I just told you my point. You will get caught either way.'

'No, I get that. But what I don't get is why you have to point out to us that we will get caught in the end. Somehow, it feels as though you really want us to get caught.'

I'm lost. They're, like, talking in riddles. They're just spinning out with their words, but they all mean the same.

'And why would I want you to get caught?' Laya frowns.

'Because you hate us? You want us gone? You wish you never met us? I don't know! I can't read your mind!' Faye exclaims exasperatedly.

'I can't believe this,' Laya whispers to herself before speaking up, almost as if she's letting out all her pent up frustration, 'Haven't you considered that maybe I just want to help you out?'

For the umpteenth time since we met Laya, we are once again stunned into silence.

She looks ashamed about her outburst and says quietly, 'Sorry about that.'

'That's okay,' I say when I see that none of my friends wish to speak with her or even be close to her.

She looks at me—the only one willing to listen to what she has to say—and speaks, 'You really should not go out there right now. You will immediately be captured and your mission to reach that woman will be unsuccessful, not to mention that getting all the way here will have been pointless. It will all have been for nothing.'

I frown. 'Why the sudden change of mind? You didn't look like you wanted to help us out before.'

'I came to my senses,' she says truthfully.

'And you expect us to believe that? Just because you have come back to your senses, you want us to believe that you are a good person? Is that what you are trying to say?' Faye spits out.

I glare at Faye and she rolls her eyes. Can't my friends just move past it all and act mature in this dire situation? Now that I think about it, we have been doing nothing much but arguing. We argue every time we have the chance and with everyone we can.

'I know you don't know who I am,' Laya says calmly, 'but trust me. I want to help you out. I listened to your story from Aeni last night. She told me how and why you came here to meet Mahsuri—I mean, Permaisuri.'

She winced as she said her name.

'I know, I heard.' Faye maintains her composure, but I know she's burning up with anger inside.

She heard us last night? To what extent? The whole thing?

I ignore her and ask Laya, 'You really want to help us? Even though you are opposed to the idea of us meeting with the Permaisuri?'

'To a certain extent. But yes, I'll try my best to help you.'

'How can we know that you truly want to help us? You're probably taking advantage of us and leading us straight to her.' Faye speaks angrily.

'For the last time, might I remind you that I will never do that!'

'Can you guys please stop arguing? I've already heard this conversation before!' Nihal asks. He pulls up a chair and sits down. 'Are we going or not? My head is pounding with a headache and you guys are making it all worse. Plus, my feet hurt.'

'You know he's right. We haven't stopped arguing ever since it all began as though we've been cursed or something,' Indra says, taking a seat beside Nihal.

'That's nonsense, of course we have not been cursed. There is no such thing as that,' Faye reprimands.

'Stop acting so foolish, Nihal. Just like Faye said, there is no such thing as being cursed.' Indra nudges his elbow and turns to me, 'So, have we come up with a decision yet? Are we staying or are we going right now?'

They all turn to look at me, even Laya, and I sigh. 'Why are you guys looking at me? I'm not the leader here. We make decisions by voting or what the majority agrees upon. This is a democracy.'

Laya snickers and I look at her, annoyed. 'Do you have a problem with how we make decisions too? Is everything annoying to you? Is that it?'

'I didn't even say anything,' Laya holds her arms up defensively. 'You're the one jumping to conclusions about me. In fact, that's all you've done to me ever since we met. I don't know if it's bad luck or what, but I'd really appreciate it if you'd stop.'

'I thought we decided to stop arguing?' Nihal stands up to showcase his sense of urgency. 'This is seriously getting ridiculous.'

'So, what do you guys think we should do? Let's vote on it,' I say.

Faye murmurs to herself, 'It's like we're a part of the council or something.'

I am about to yell at her when Indra stops me and gives me a look that says *you better not start*. 'Aeni! Seriously, enough!'

'Whatever.' Nihal rolls his eyes and slumps down on the chair.

'If you're done nagging.' I stare at Indra before continuing, 'Let's vote. Those in favour of heading outside now?'

No one raises their hands in favour of the suggestion so I continue, 'Those in favour of staying in the shack and heading out later in the evening or when the situation outside eases up or any form of the military activity halts?'

Everyone raises their hands in the air, including me.

'For once, we agree on one thing.' Nihal smiles at each one of us. 'If we're done here, I want to go and take a short nap for a while.'

He heads to the living room, which we have turned into our fort for the night. Faye follows suit behind him and is also followed by Indra, who keeps gazing at Laya and I back and forth as if silently saying *I'm watching you*.

In the dimly lit corridor that leads to the front door, Laya and I stand, staring into each other's eyes, wondering what the other might do next.

# Chapter 21

Laya stares out the window situated next to the front door and silence consumes the corridor. I turn to see what she's looking at but there's apparently nothing out there to see other than trees swaying in the breeze, the orange-tinted sky, and a few birds zooming past to the land beyond.

I break the silence, 'What made you change your mind to help us?'

She looks at me for a fleeting second before turning her gaze back to the window. 'It's what someone dear to me would tell me to do in this kind of situation.'

She looks like she's ready to move the conversation along to another topic so I don't push the question further. Instead, I ask something that I have been curious to ask, 'What does it feel like to live in the castle?'

'Dark, looming, and boring probably best describe my time spent cooped up in there. It's why I'd rather live here alone than in there. Even though the place is filled with human beings in every nook and cranny, the palace seems lifeless, as though joy has been sucked and thrown far away.'

I can't even begin to imagine what that must feel like. Even though I only live with Ma, it's always been fun and never dull for us, even when it's only the two of us. I feel like I can talk to her about everything, and I'm not ashamed to admit it. Even when we have little disagreements that turn into arguments, one of us always makes amends. Ma is like my best friend, and I wouldn't trade her for the world. I wish she was here with me.

'That sounds frustrating. It must've been hard on you,' I state it out loud. 'What about your parents? Do you have any siblings? How were you even assigned to work in the palace? You seem to be around my age—shouldn't you still be down at the Academy, training and learning for the job you will soon be assigned and work in for the rest of your life?'

She takes a breath at the mention of her family and a look of sadness spreads across her face.

'Why does that matter to you?'

I am taken aback by her question. 'These are questions you ask someone who you would like to get closer with. Like friends, for example. Wouldn't you be asking those questions if we were friends?'

'You're not my friend.'

'Okay then. It was worth a shot.' I bet she doesn't even have any friends with the way she's closing herself off to other people. I don't bother asking any other questions because I know I won't get any answers out of her, but I try one last time, for the sake of our freedom out of this complicated situation. 'Will you help us get to the palace? You're familiar with it and know your way around. That's all we're asking of you, and we will be out of your sight before you know it.'

The look on her face shows me nothing of her reaction—it's completely blank. So, I try again. 'Look, I know we have done nothing but bother you ever since we met down at the station, and I know you desperately want to get rid of us. I swear, this is the last time you'll see any of us. We will leave you alone after this.'

She sighs before walking away, heading down the corridor. She turns her head to the side before saying, 'Come on. You said you guys are a team. I'm sure the others would like to hear the plan too.'

Is she actually being nice right now? What a sudden turn of events!

When Laya and I step into the room, Indra sits up, Faye looks unfazed while Nihal continues laying on his back, under the covers.

'Come on, guys! It's time we plan this through and make it work,' I say encouragingly, hoping that it'll lighten their spirits. But, of course, my friends remain the same even when I have given them my biggest smile. I almost feel deflated, but what good will that do? It's better to be all smiles and happy against three unrelenting and wallowing souls.

'What now, Aeni?' Nihal sits up and pushes the covers aside, 'I was just about to take a nap. Why did you have to come in here and disrupt the peace?'

Laya gives him a bored look. 'You have no time to be taking a nap with the situation you're currently in. As a matter of fact, you don't even have the time to be complaining.'

I interrupt before they start arguing and it'll just take us nowhere, 'I hereby ban anyone from starting an argument or even getting anywhere near it. The ban commences as of this moment.'

'Stop trying to be so dramatic.' Nihal lies down on his back and pulls the cover up to his face so it covers him whole.

'Guys, seriously! We need to start planning. We were even blessed with a guide to take us around the island! Doesn't that sound like something else?' I start, but my friends remain the same. Now I feel like breaking the ban that I just made if this is the reaction I get from them!

'Can you guys at least be more cooperative and take part in this? Why do I have to constantly feel as though I'm the only one who wants to get out of this alive? You guys are just too much sometimes! It's no wonder I have to lead this so-called group most of the time!' I sigh and slightly pull my hair in frustration.

Indra actually looks guilty and stares at the ground. Faye still looks unfazed while Nihal is still trying to hide under the covers. I look at Laya when she snickers and lean on the wall. She shrugs and gives me a look like she can't help it.

'If you guys are going to be this insufferable, we might as well just part our ways. Faye, you can just go back to the Central Island, head home and announce everything to the authorities for all I care! Nihal, you can just do whatever the hell you want. I'm so sick and tired of this!' I add as I turn around and say to Laya, 'Are you still up to be the guide?'

'I guess. Whatever.'

'Great! Because I'm in.' I am about to leave the room when Indra stops me. He stands up and places his arm on one of my shoulders, 'Aeni! Wait!'

I don't turn around and manage to say in a calm manner, 'What?'

'I'm sorry, man. I don't know what came over me. I think I'm still shocked with what happened yesterday at the station. Sometimes, I just can't wrap my mind around the idea of where we are now, what we're doing, and the reason for it all. Sometimes, it just feels like a dream that feels so real. I have to make myself believe that this is real. This is indeed happening. And I am fully awake.'

I sigh when I hear his explanation. 'You think I don't feel the same way? I do, I can't help it that I do. We just have to take charge and show everyone who's boss.'

'Aeni!' I turn around when Nihal calls me. He has finally gotten out of the covers and has a determined look on his face. 'First of all, if you expect me to explain why we have been so, in your words, insufferable then you're not going to get that from me. It'll take more than that to crack me and get me to pour out what has been pent up inside me since all that has happened in the last few days. Seriously, don't expect it.' He smiles at me and continues, 'My leg hurts so much, and I just feel like bursting out in anger at everyone. Don't expect me to pour my heart out like you did, Indra. I'm not a wimp.'

I couldn't even muster enough anger to hate him for his candour. I'm just glad that we can get this all out, once and, hopefully, for all.

This is good. This is healthy. Get all those pent up emotions out of the way and look forward to our next step.

'But for what it's worth, I'm sorry,' Nihal adds and gives me a warm smile. He tries to walk up to me and hug me.

'I'm sorry too,' I place my arms around his waist.

Indra snickers, 'Now, who's a wimp?'

One day, I'm going to replay this moment right here. One day . . .

'So, we should probably start the plan now if we're ever going to make a breakthrough.' Nihal pats my shoulder and winces at his every move. He moves to sit down on his makeshift bed.

I lock my eyes on Faye, and she nods at me, looking nowhere else but at me. She must still be mad at me for continuously repeating what she has said in the past. Sometimes, I just have a feeling that what I often tell her out of anger is actually true to how she feels deep inside her.

'Are you guys done making up?' Laya smirks as she tilts her head to the side.

'Yes, thank you very much,' Nihal says as fast as he can and looks away, embarrassed.

I look at each one of them, 'Shall we finally and officially begin the plan now?'

# Chapter 22

'Wait, so are you actually saying that not even the military has memorized the tunnels like you have, like the back of your hand?' Nihal asks Laya for yet another round of confirmation, certainly in amazement and wonder.

'Is there even a map of the tunnels?' Faye adds.

'The important army officials have maps. Like the general or the ones who hold a higher rank in the army, but even they're too lazy to memorize it. They don't often use the tunnels unless it is absolutely necessary, since they can just walk on land.'

'Wait, are there creatures down there?' Nihal looks intimidated by the idea.

'Of course not. Those are just scary tales the army officers tell to scare one another, especially at night.' Laya looks amused by their incessant questions. She's finally being her true self. Her outer skin of pretence seems to have come off, and she looks more carefree.

By now, we have finally decided on a plan that we think is best, even Laya thinks that it's not a bad idea, that it could work. But we also can't be too hopeful about the outcome, as we still don't know what awaits us once we reach our destination—the royal palace. We're now waiting for the time to pass as we wait for dusk to end. As soon as the sun sets and more of the army officers are no longer roaming down the tunnels, we will be on our way to the palace. Laya has also briefed us on the route that will take us inside. She didn't go into too much detail because who can take in all those left and right turns? Not me and not my friends either. Laya stopped as soon as she saw the blank look on our faces as she was telling us to take the third left turn. She realized this exercise was pointless and just asked us to not veer away and to stay close behind her.

We are going to knock down the military, which will no doubt try to block our way, and ambush the Permaisuri's chamber. We really are maniacs for actually attempting to do this. We're probably going to be sentenced to the most punishable act of the High Law—death for endangering the Permaisuri's as well as others' safety. I try not to think too much about the consequences and instead focus on the fact that this might be our only chance to make her hear what we have to say for ourselves.

Faye snaps me out of my reverie, and I am finally listening to their conversation as she asks, 'How did you have the time to memorize the maze-like ways that are the tunnels?'

'I had a lot of time to spare.'

Faye nods and asks another question, 'Were you raised in the palace?'

Laya looks far off. 'You can say that.'

'What was it like?'

Laya smiles before sneaking a glance at me, 'Dark, looming, and boring.'

I can't help but smile as I remember the words she said the night before. I feel a sense of victory, knowing more about her than my friends have had the chance to find out.

'Enough about me,' Laya announces. 'What about you guys? What is it like to live on Central Island with everyone else?'

'I guess you can just say that it's totally normal for us. Nothing exciting ever happens. We'd wake up in the morning with the announcement on the speakers, head to the Academy on the tram, study and train for what we have been assigned to do for the rest of our lives. After we're done with the Academy for the day, we go back to our own domiciles or some days we hang out together, have our dinner, and head to bed for the day. The next day, it happens all over again. Didn't I tell you it was boring?' Faye explains and now that I've heard her speak about our daily lives, it finally sinks in for me that we do live a very dull life, and there's nothing we can do to elevate it.

We'd probably have died without going on an adventure if we weren't stuck in this situation and the thought makes me sad.

Faye continues, 'Except for the recent turn of events, where things got slightly exciting for us. We can't say we're lucky to be able to witness it because then we wouldn't have been in this situation. Forget that, what happened was everyone was being controlled as soon as they were injected with some substance. Everyone turned into a robot and became lifeless—nothing like human beings with emotions that we are born with. Except this didn't happen to us.'

'So, are you guys special that you can overcome the influence of that substance?' Laya can't help but wonder.

'No,' I say, 'I think we missed the first shot they gave. Nothing special, we were just in another place at the exact moment it all happened. Can't say our families got lucky.'

Laya nods and doesn't ask any other questions, as the light outside is slowly turning a darker tint of orange, replacing the clouds and the starless sky with darkness.

*Sunset*.

Everyone goes quiet as we see the sun set in the distance and the possibilities that await us.

It's time to go.

For the next few minutes, everyone minds their own business in silence, but it does nothing to water down the nervousness that I'm feeling inside. I'm sure the others feel the same way too.

'Is everyone good to go?' I ask and in return, every one of my friends give me indistinctive murmurs, too preoccupied to respond properly.

I look around the living area to spot Faye, but she's not here. I walk out of the room heading to the kitchen and there, in the corner, stands the lone figure that I'm looking for. Faye is tending to her supplies that she can bring with her inside her rucksack, and I walk towards her. She hasn't uttered a word since I spoke badly to her a few hours ago and it has been niggling at my conscious. She didn't deserve that and it's time for me to make amends.

'Faye, I'm sorry,' I start, 'I didn't mean to say what I said. I was angry, and I just blurted it out.'

She continues to ignore me, and I pull my hair back in frustration. You never know what's running around their minds and what they're thinking about. For all I know, she's already thinking of a thousand ways to kill me already.

I yelp at the thought and apologize again, 'Faye? I really didn't mean it. I shouldn't even have those kinds of thoughts. I'm really sorry.'

'But you just can't help it that you do. I get it. You have nothing to apologize about. After all, isn't everyone entitled to their own opinion and judgement?' She says in a clipped tone.

'Faye, please! I really did not mean it and I am truly, deeply, and regretfully sorry.'

She shoves her handheld gun down into her backpack with more force than necessary. 'There's nothing you can do about it now. Let's just move on, shall we?'

I refuse to relent to her wishes, 'I'm afraid I can't move on until you forgive me.'

She stares at me defiantly, but I don't concede. She can be very intimidating sometimes but not this time. I refuse to back down. 'Please, Faye? Will you please forgive me?' I plead.

She zips her rucksack and slings it on her shoulders. She's about to walk away, but I block her way.

Faye looks annoyed. 'Aeni, move! Everyone else is waiting.'

I shake my head and stand taller, 'Only if you forgive me.'

From back in the living area comes Indra's voice, yelling for us to hurry up.

I remain firm. 'Come on, Faye. You don't want to be the reason we're all late and ruin our plan.'

She sighs. 'Fine.'

My ears perk up, expectant. 'I won't move until I hear the words coming out of your mouth that you forgive me.'

She looks at me and finally caves. 'Fine! I forgive you. Are you happy now? And can we go now?'

I stand aside so that she can rejoin our friends and as she walks away, I can hear her mumbling to herself jokingly. 'Pain in the ass.'

As we step into the living area, Indra asks, 'What took you guys so long?'

I shrug while Faye says begrudgingly, 'Don't ask me.'

I lock eyes with Laya, who is giving me a look I can't quite decipher. Before I can ask her, Faye announces, 'We should go now! Laya, please lead the way.'

Laya nods, cracks open the door leading to the tunnels down below, and disappears. My friends go down one by one. I'm the last one to go as I stare at the shack one last time, hoping that this feeling I'm experiencing right now will not be the last time I feel safe in a momentary sanctuary and haven.

# PART IV

# Chapter 23

'This is it,' Laya stops. I'm not sure how long we've been down in these tunnels because it seems as though time has stood still. She finally points towards a ceiling and this time, a ladder is placed against the wall. 'This will take you straight into the royal palace's wet kitchen. By this time, everyone will have already gone to bed and the area should be clear.'

We are staring at one another, waiting and hoping that someone is going to volunteer to go up first but no one does. We look nervous, and Laya is not able to pick up our feelings as she frowns at us. 'What are you waiting for?'

'Shouldn't you be heading up first?' Faye asks, and if I know my friend well enough, I know she's hoping that Laya will go first to assess the place for us.

Laya laughs in disbelief. 'You have got to be kidding me. The plan was only for me to guide you through the tunnels. I never agreed to guide you through the palace as well. What I have done is already good enough. This is as far as I can go with you.'

'Is that how it is now?' Faye looks annoyed, still trying to make her go first.

'You're on your own now.' Laya hooks her arms down under her chest.

We look at one another and have a silent conversation, made possible by the many years we've been friends. I am dreading that Laya might have led us straight to the tiger's den. So far, she has done nothing to make us suspicious, but I can't be too sure. Who knows what's waiting for us up there if she is just sending us off?

But Faye has already decided by herself. 'Then I guess we owe you a thank you and a farewell. Goodbye.' Faye doesn't wait for her reply as she climbs up the ladder.

I watch her silently disappear from my view, and my heart starts thumping loudly. Is she okay? But her face appears above us, and she gives a reassuring smile. 'There's no one here. All clear. You can come up.'

Nihal goes next. He only manages a nod before climbing up while struggling with his leg and disappearing above. Indra is the only one who musters a timid smile before whispering, 'Thank you and goodbye.'

It is just me and Laya now. I assume the area must be clear as was promised since I don't hear any call of distress from any of my friends above. The girl standing in front of me nods before turning around and walking away.

*So much for a farewell.*

I am about to call her out before Indra whispers, his head peeking out from the hole, 'Aeni, are you coming?'

I say, 'Yeah. In a minute.'

'You know what she said was right. Just let her go. Our original plan has always been just the four of us.' Faye admonishes.

I climb up the ladder with ease and close it behind me. Indra is right. The four of us will stick together, no matter what happens. I'm not going to risk it by chasing after someone who clearly wants to spend the rest of her life alone. Besides, what would be the point?

We immediately move on with our plan and venture into the palace. This is the first time any one of us has ever seen such rich and posh surroundings in every corner of a building, and we can't help but feel mesmerized by it.

Faye, who has the best memory out of us all, leads the way Laya has briefed us will take us in the direction of the Permaisuri's chamber. I take a moment to get accustomed to the idea of us being in the palace, but once I step out of the kitchen, I have to wrap my head around the idea again as I take in every single detail of the interior.

Since the kitchen is in the lower ground while the Permaisuri's chamber is two floors above, we have to make our way around the palace, hoping to spot a flight of stairs. According to Laya, there are a total of four sets of stairs—one is for general use, which is also the one the Permaisuri uses, the maids use the one that is situated at the back of the palace, one is for the army to navigate around where they're stationed easily, and finally there is one not everyone who works in the palace knows about. It is a special flight of stairs that leads down the basement and to the dungeon.

We enter a long corridor, which will lead us to the specialized stairs for the maids, since it will be easier to tackle down maids rather than the army. It's bound to happen anyway if we're going to ambush the Permaisuri—that part I am certainly aware of.

'Are we heading in the right direction?' Indra whispers.

Faye nods while glancing around, 'It should be around here somewhere . . . there!'

She points to the right and true to Laya's words, there is a flight of stairs that can lead us all the way up to the top floor. We climb up as quietly as we can for fear of someone hearing the rickety stairs before we face one of the army officers.

We stop as we reach the last step of the second floor, as though we can read each other's minds, and say to ourselves, *This is it. We're really doing this. There's no turning back now.*

'Hey! What are you doing here? You—'

He is knocked out cold by Faye's strong punch, and we stare at her in disbelief. She shrugs like it really isn't a big deal. 'We can't stop somewhere for too long. We need to constantly keep moving.'

We nod and make our way to our designated destination. We are stopped by a few army officers and stealthily knock them down. Stealthily would be an exaggeration, it is more like don't think twice, just act and knock them down however we can. What do you expect? We're just newbies, and we don't have miraculous force and experience against these guys. At the Academy, my aptitude test result came out to be categorized under Group D along with Nihal and Indra. We were trained to become factory workers, shopkeepers, cleaners, and others that fall under the same category—not for combat or battle.

I want to let out a deep breath that I never realized I was holding in, but I'll be lying and manipulating myself. We haven't even successfully breached the Permaisuri's chamber, only spotted the door to it from three doors away while hiding behind the crevice of a wall.

Faye counts the number of army officers we have to tackle down next. 'There are at least eight of them stationed in front of the chamber. And we don't even know if there are any inside the room with her.'

I have to muster up all my energy to do this, and I'm already half weary, with all my energy burned out. Man, I feel so weak right now. If I was offered and given the chance to train in combat, remind me to not even think twice and to just grab it.

'Someone should distract them,' Indra whispers.

'No!' Nihal protests in defiance, 'We should stick together.'

'What other choice do we have?' Indra whispers back aggressively, 'This is our only chance.'

Nihal argues, 'Whoever stays behind will be a slaughtered lamb, already knowing their only fate is death. There's no way the one who is left behind will make it out alive.'

In a way, I understand clearly where he is coming from. It was either all or none.

'Enough!' Faye grumbles, 'We stick together and we fight them off together and everyone will make it into that chamber, alive. We mustn't be selfish in this situation. If we help one another, we can make sure that each of us makes it in there alive.'

I feel proud of her, but I don't let it show. Besides, this isn't the time to marvel over how cool my friend is. 'Does everyone agree with this plan?' I say and they all nod. Their expressions have changed, full of determination and drive.

*We can do this.* I repeat to myself over and over again as we stand side by side in a line, exposed to the army officer's peripheral vision.

One of them yells out, 'Who's there?'

'Come take a closer look if you're curious,' Nihal taunts them, and they do as we tell them to, all eight of them. The bait is hooked. What is left for us to do is yank them out of the water and into the relentless grasp of our fists.

I stand closer to Faye as we split the group in two: Faye is with me and Indra is grouped with Nihal. And off we go, punching and kicking whichever one of them would come in our way. It feels surreal to go one on one against the army officers but perhaps because of the experience from before, we work in tandem to tackle them one at a time.

After what feels like hours, I finally knock one down as another one comes over and we take turns punching him in the face. My opponent is caught off guard, as I kick his leg with everything I have in me and punch him right on his face. I hear a crunching sound and the man yelps in pain, walking away from me.

That's right. One point for me and zero points for him. I steal a glance from the corner of my eye as I gaze to see how Faye is doing. She seems fine on her own. Every time one of them comes close to her, she knees them right in their manhood. She doesn't even need my help if you ask me. That must hurt, though. I feel bad for them but I don't.

Nihal and Indra are both tackling a man, and it definitely looks like the fight is in their favour. Despite Nihal's injury yesterday, he makes it up with the sheer force of his determination. Faye and I run towards the chamber and I unbolt the doors. I would not have managed to do that if the doors were locked, but thanks to my luck, they weren't.

The room is spacious and, during the day, sunlight would stream into the room and brighten up the whole chamber. Some usual furniture decorates the room, but I don't give them a second thought as my gaze lands on a lone figure sitting on the four-poster bed.

'Who are you?' she asks, her voice serene yet with a hint of hostility. There's a sheer cover on every side of the four-poster bed, so we don't have a good view of the woman we have risked so much to talk to.

'We have come to talk to you,' I say, my voice commanding.

'Why should I have to hear to what you have to say?' She bursts out, hands gesturing wide.

'Because—' I start responding but am interrupted when Nihal and Indra barge into the room. I'm glad they're okay, just a slight bruise here and there. I continue trying to remain calm. 'We have been falsely accused and we want to turn everything back to normal—to the way things were before all the citizens started acting like robots. Before getting into anything else, explain to us why they're being controlled?'

She refuses. 'You have come to talk and persuade the wrong person here. I simply do not know what you are talking about.'

Faye interjects, 'Surely you know! You are the Permaisuri of the city of Killen. You rule these lands! How can you say that you have no idea what we are talking about? Do you actually expect us to believe what you just said? Like fools?'

The Permaisuri is moving from her position and seems to be making her way towards us. Even the way she's walking is regal, like she didn't just wake up from slumber. As she comes closer to us, we see that she has on pink satin pyjamas, her black hair is swishing side to side as she moves. I have never been so close to her and take all of her in. She doesn't look old at all, she looks to be about only a few years older than us. Nothing like the photograph that I always walk past at the Academy.

I know that no one would like to get caught admitting it, but she is actually beautiful in her own way, now that I've taken a closer look at her. She also doesn't look as intimidating as she lets on. She just looks like a young woman who really knows what she is doing.

'Tell me.' She stops in front of them, scrutinizing each one of them. 'Who has falsely accused you? And to what extent does it involve Killen's High Law?'

I begin, standing tall as she locks her gaze on me, 'They have accused us of being traitors to the—'

'Who are these "they" you keep referring to?' the Permaisuri interrupts me.

'The army officers who were commanded to capture us. And a general too,' I confess.

She frowns. 'I see.'

Nihal suddenly yells out, 'They chased us and we had to hide away from them. Even the citizens were joining the chase to capture us.'

She gives us a blank look. 'This all doesn't make sense to me. I wish to believe you but—'

The Permaisuri stops, looking behind us, and whispers, 'Anista?'

I turn around and try to make out who it is from their shadow before it sinks in.

It's Laya.

# Chapter 24

Nihal breaks into a smile seeing an ally, 'Laya! You came back!'

The Permaisuri's face is pale as though she just saw a ghost walking around the hall, 'Anista, what are you doing here?'

I frown as the Permaisuri utters that name again. Is she seeing double? Does she think that Laya is actually someone else she knows? After all, why would she be on a first name basis with a maid? It doesn't make any sense to me.

'That's Laya, right?' Nihal whispers to Faye, and she nods. The person standing there in the entryway of the chamber is undoubtedly the girl we first met in the tunnels down below—the girl who helped us trudge through the underground tunnels and straight into the palace. We wouldn't be here right now if it weren't for her.

'What kind of a question is that?' Laya counter-attacks with a stoic reply.

'It was a sensible question. One that made me curious about where you were wandering around the palace.'

'I can't even wander about in my own home? What? Do you expect me to stay cooped up in my bedroom every hour of the day? What am I? A prisoner?'

'That's not what I meant.' The Permaisuri sighs. 'But from what I have found out, you haven't been staying in this palace. You've been wandering around down in the tunnels down below.'

'And why is that any of your concern?' Laya's gaze doesn't stray away from the Permaisuri's, and I want to check if this girl is being serious. She seems to have no fear, and it's making me worry for her.

*Hold on, is there something I'm missing here?*

'It is all of my concern. You are my responsibility now, ever since—'

'I've heard enough!' Laya snaps before the Permaisuri can continue her sentence.

The four of us are just standing there in the middle of their argument, and I am actually contemplating if we should move or leave or stay? It just feels odd to be here, listening into their conversation, which ultimately should be held in private. Is it just me or do they really know each other? But how could they be related to one another? Friend? Distant relatives? Or Laya is, after all, a mere maid? The latter is unlikely, since I know a maid would never dare to talk back to the Permaisuri's face let alone look her in the eye.

'Anista,' the Permaisuri's voice is calm and loving as she takes little steps towards Laya, 'please for once, just listen to me. I know you think the worst of me; that you loathe me. Over time, I have grown accustomed to this fact. But I just want you to know that there never was and there never will be a time when I have felt any negative feelings towards you. I wish we could go back to how things were before. I never intended for any of this to happen and I am forevermore sorry.'

Both their eyes are brimming with tears now, and I still can't place what their relationship is with one another and the extent of it.

Laya blinks the tears away and says in a cold voice, 'There's nothing you can do now. It is—'

'Fine. I am done here. This stops now. Me being sorry for something I was not even responsible for. Don't come to me later and say that you regret your decisions when you actually find out the truth. You just want to find someone to blame and I am the only one who you can find to blame it on!'

Laya stands on guard, unyielding, 'I'm leaving. For good. And I'm never coming back.'

The Permaisuri looks resigned and stares at her feet. 'Do whatever you want. Leave before the guards find something wrong and alarm the whole island.'

I am about to argue my way in when Laya demands, 'And leave the four of them alone. They have done nothing wrong. If you have any conscience left, you will let them be.'

The Permaisuri nods and walks towards the floor-to-ceiling glass panel door that slides open onto the balcony outside. 'I will see what I can do.'

I hear footsteps faintly coming from the hall and down below. The Permaisuri looks in our direction, her lips a thin line. 'Go now.'

I nod and announce to my friends, who are staring around, mouths agape at the turn of events. 'We need to go. Hurry!'

We walk briskly out of the chamber, the last I see of the Permaisuri is her gazing up at the moon and the night sky that looms over the landscape. We stop after seeing the incoming tide of army officers to our left and right. They don't look like they're about to stop.

I look behind my back and spot Laya still standing where she has been ever since she arrived, staring longingly at the figure by the window, knowing that it's the last time they're ever going to see each other again. I know saying goodbye and all that is hard, but we don't have time for it right now. I snap at her to grab her attention. 'Come on! We need to go!'

They are slowly advancing on us, and there's no way we can escape now.

An incredibly intimidating and commanding voice orders the army officers to halt. 'Let them go. This is an order from the Permaisuri, by refusing to do so, you will be facing grave consequences.'

We turn around and look at the Permaisuri, who is charged up by the ordeal. We run away as fast as we can from the scene, fearful that she might realize what a foolish decision she has just made. She would probably demand for us to be captured and held in the dungeon for all eternity.

I feel as though I am flying away from danger, relieved yet wondering what made her let us go. But still relieved, nonetheless. Could it be that the Permaisuri's relationship with Laya didn't make her hesitate about her decision?

Laya is guiding us without us asking her to do so. We are once again in the tunnels and careening right and left wherever Laya's headed while we follow her closely behind. I don't see or hear anyone following behind us, and I continue walking ahead.

We reach the train station, and Laya doesn't stop or slow down. She continues into the already opened doors of the train. My friends hesitate for a while before heading inside, but I stop right at the edge of where the train and the platform connects.

'Aeni? What are you doing? Get inside!' Indra screeches.

'We're leaving the island?' I ask even though I know the answer to it.

'Of course, we are. Why else would we board the train? Seriously, what are you doing? We need to go!' Indra rushes me.

I don't question them anymore and step into the coach. The doors shut completely behind me, and I slump on one of the seats as the train starts to move.

I need a minute to let all of this sink in!

'I can't believe we actually did it!' Nihal jumps in glee, 'But are we clear of the accusation? Are we free to go back home? Are we no longer fugitives? Where do we stand now? What are we going to do now?'

I furrow my brow. 'Even though we've met the Permaisuri, I still feel like there are more questions that have arisen than I ever wondered about before. Have we accomplished what we came here to do? Are we really free? Who knows, am I right?'

'Who cares? I can't believe we even made it out of the palace in one piece!' Indra whoops in joy by the rush of adrenaline.

'Did you guys know what happened to the two of them back there? It sounded really heated!' I try to tone down my volume a notch, genuinely curious.

'That was really something else,' Nihal agrees. 'I didn't know what to do and what to make of everything I was hearing at the time. It felt like I was an intruder given the situation we were in.'

'Do you guys know who she truly is?' Faye suddenly speaks up and points in the direction of Laya who is in the other carriage, alone.

'Who is she?' Indra asks, seriously. The joy that is seeping into our carriage is momentarily sucked away.

'You haven't figured it out yet?' Faye asks.

I shake my head.

'She's Anista Laya,' Faye says quietly. 'The Permaisuri's younger sister.'

# Chapter 25

'You can't be serious!' Nihal exclaims, 'Then how have we never heard of her before?'

'She likes to be hidden away from society, like she wants nothing do with the royal family or anyone for the matter.' Faye explains.

My need to know of their relationship has been answered and it all makes sense now—why she has the gall to be disrespectful towards the Permaisuri and even the way they fought and argued. Could it be all just be a sisters' brawl? The context remains unclear to me.

'Was she purposely hidden away by the Permaisuri or was it by choice?' Indra frowns at the thought.

Now that I think about it, she does have the glow and regal aura of a royal family. From the way she moves to the way she speaks, the use of her language is definitely more extravagant than ordinary. No matter how hard she tries to run away from it, it'll always be a part of her. It's in her genes. She is, after all, the next one in line for the throne. There's no one else who can take over her position and replace her. There is no one who is more qualified than her.

They must be each other's only relative because any other family members they may have are unheard of.

'I don't know about that. But what I do know is that something terrible happened a few years back but no one knows the actual truth behind it. Remember the news of both the king and queen who had died at the same time? How old were we back then? It was around eight years ago, so at the time, we must have been around eight?' She pauses before continuing, 'Doesn't it sound suspicious to any of you guys too?'

'Hold on a minute there,' Indra looks at Faye suspiciously, 'How do you even know that Laya is her sister? And also, no one dares to talk about the previous king and queen. Especially not now when she's right there.'

'I just put two and two together. Piece by piece we can put together a whole and that can make the whole story one big picture.'

'For someone who coincidentally put two and two together, you sure seem to know a lot. How did you even know about all this?' I cut in.

'Why are you guys trying to gang up on me? I'm just saying stuff that I have heard and read about in the library,' Faye retorts.

'But such information is not available to the public. We just don't know about it, end of story.' Indra still sounds suspicious about whatever it is that Faye knows. Sometimes, she can act like a whole different person yet she tries so hard to be herself. It's confusing and even suspicious.

Faye continues, clearly frustrated, 'You know what? I can't even say anything without feeling discriminated. You just want to make anything that is out of the ordinary seem like something that is wrong but it's not.'

'Did your dad tell you about this?' Nihal exclaims, trying to justify his friend, looking delighted by the inventiveness of his idea. 'It only makes sense. Your dad could have accidentally told you this information or you could have read a document regarding all this? Your dad, after all, holds a high rank in the army. This is the only explanation. Am I right, Faye?'

Faye is taken aback before finally succumbing. 'You're right. I once read his mission reports when he wasn't looking, and sometimes I'd even read them when he wasn't home.'

'You could've just told us that!' Nihal nudges their elbows together. 'We're your friends after all.'

'Right, of course. But I could be in trouble if my dad found out that I read his reports, so it was better for me to keep it a secret to myself. It was safer that way.'

Indra adds, 'There's no use trying to hide it from us. In time, the truth will come out and nothing is going to stop it.'

What Indra just said has really struck to me. The look that Faye is trying hard to maintain adds up to my confusion even more. Is there really something else that she's hiding from us? If yes, I need to know.

Nihal yawns loudly, 'I'm tired. I'm going to snooze, if you don't mind.' He lies down in the middle of the carriage and tosses and turns until he finds a comfortable position. He holds his head up, 'How long does this train ride take to our destination? Does anyone know?'

'We'll arrive there in the morning. The journey will take five hours tops.' Laya steps inside the carriage we're currently in.

Although the most sensible way to act around her would be like how we have been treating her ever since we met, it's hard now that we know her true identity—her true value on this island. She was like a hidden gem among a thousand rocks.

We stare at her, barely blinking as she walks to the front of the car and makes her way around the control system of the train.

'Do you guys think she heard us?' Nihal asks, sitting up. 'I hope she didn't. We're already in enough trouble as it is, and she was just warming up to us.'

'Shh, shut up,' I say and look at him wearily. 'Weren't you about to doze off?'

'Geez, when did you get so irritable?'

I ignore him, and instead, I look at the front of the carriage where Laya is. Should I go over there and ask if she's all right? We're friends now, right? I hope we are.

I shrug the thought away, I'm sure she wants time alone and not be with someone she barely knows, invading her space and privacy. I was taught to be better than that. No matter how tempting it might be, I will give her the space that she needs and deserves.

I lie down beside Indra and he turns around on his side so he's staring at me. I sigh. 'What?'

He smiles, 'I know what you're thinking about in that big head of yours.'

'What are you talking about? What kind of nonsense are you sputtering now?'

It seems nice that there is still a semblance of normalcy, and we can still joke around.

He chuckles and I turn away so that he's facing my back. 'Come on, talk to me. I'm bored here. Could you spare me your company or I'll go talk to Laya instead.'

I lie on my back, still refusing to look at him. 'Please! You'd never.'

We remain silent for a while until Indra says, 'Stop overthinking so much. Everything is going to be okay. We got each other. What's the worst that can happen?'

'If you say so,' I say in a singsong voice before murmuring, 'I hope so too.'

Though, despite his reassurance, I'm still not that confident.

I let my mind roam around to the land beyond—to where we're headed. My mind doesn't roam for too long as I fall asleep inside the moving train, underwater. The sound of the train moving is soothing, it's like listening to raindrops from inside my domicile.

* * *

'Aeni! Wake up!' Faye jolts me awake a little too forcefully.

She walks away and when she's far enough, as far as she can get in this train, I finally sit up. I groan as my back and shoulders sting in pain. I must have slept in a bad position through the night, and now my body has to pay for it. Great. Just great. It's just the thing I needed before heading out for the day of yet another battle of 'do whatever you have to do so long as you don't get yourself killed'. Note my sarcasm, won't you?

'Are we almost there?' I yawn and rub the hint of sleep off my face.

'Yeah, almost there,' Indra replies.

'Guys, look!' Nihal says as he stares outside.

The train is coming out of the water and it doesn't stop as it zooms atop the water on the track. From a distance, it must look like the train is travelling not on a track but on water. It must be a sight to behold from afar.

Indra says in an excited tone, almost screaming, 'Forget about that! Look at that!'

I stand beside Indra and look where he is with so much fascination, and when I see what is standing proudly in front of me, where our destination is situated, I am left speechless.

There, standing as high as it can go is a massive wall that reaches up to the sky. And the only thing on my mind is how are we really going to escape the island? Is it possible?

# Chapter 26

Even before the train arrives, from this distance, we can already see the military stationed outside.

'What . . . are they waiting for us?' Nihal panics.

'No,' Laya closes the door to the control room. 'Even without danger, they have always been stationed there. Basic protocol of the island, since no one is allowed to leave the city.'

'Like a precaution?' Faye asks for confirmation.

'Yes. A precaution from the people within and the people out there.'

Indra looks wary about the idea. 'Wait, did you just say there are other people outside Killen?'

'Yes. Did you expect that we are the only ones left in the world? Don't be silly. The war has killed a lot of people everywhere around the world, but it hasn't killed everyone. There are still people outside of Killen, living freely.'

'What do you mean freely?' I ask.

'It means that they have no law to abide by or no leader, let alone a government, and the most crucial thing is that it is not peaceful and safe out there like Killen is.'

Faye adds, 'Yet you still want to go out there?'

'Yes.'

'How do you know about all of that?' Nihal asks, actually curious, and I look at him. Was that really a serious question? She's a royal! Of course, she knows that kind of information.

'There's no time for me to explain now. We're almost approaching,' Laya looks ahead, resting a gun on her shoulders.

'We are allowed to use weapons, right?' Indra warily holds his gun, testing the weight in his hand.

'Of course! Do you expect us to tackle those army officers unharmed while their weapons are fully stocked? If you wish to die, then that is up to you.' Laya's gaze doesn't stray as she checks the bullets and cocks the gun confidently.

Then, the rest of us take out the weapons that were safely placed inside our backpacks. I hesitantly grip mine and copy what Laya is doing—I check the bullets to make sure the gun is loaded. I never in my life expected myself to be in this situation with my friends.

Laya quickly explains how to use our weapons, just to make sure we all know how to handle them.

'Are you guys ready?' I ask, my heart is beating incessantly.

They all nod, and once again, we look at each other hard. I'm hoping against all odds that this will not be the last time that I'll see them again—that we'll live through this to tell the tale—one hell of a tale.

'Should we use the grenade now or later?' Indra points at the grenade safely encased inside the cover attached to his pants, 'It's the very last one.'

I know I told him to only bring one grenade but I am really glad he brought another one secretly. It can be the trump card for our gang, since there's so many of them and so few of us. I'm not telling him that though, I would rather not see the smug look on his face.

'Keep it for now,' Laya advices. 'We'll use it as our element of surprise.'

'Aren't we already an element of surprise?' Nihal chuckles to himself to mask his fear and when he looks at Laya's face, his joke is stolen away from him.

This is definitely not the time and place to be joking.

The train finally stops and the doors open. The closest man notices us and yells out, 'Hey! What are you doing here?'

'I wish I could answer your question first, but we have more pressing matters to attend to.' Laya smirks. She has become fiercer and more badass. 'We'll have to kill you first, if you gentlemen don't mind.'

The first shot comes from Laya, and she doesn't stop or hesitate as she charges ahead, knocking the army officers off one by one. We stay close behind her as we are soon tackling the army one head at a time, at our own pace. The nerves finally settle although my heart feels like its jumping out of my chest. I continue to do the best I can.

Whenever I victoriously manage to shoot a man down, the moment does not linger long, as I then get knocked down. I'm annoyed about this because I can see, from the corner of my eye, that the rest of them are successfully working together to bring our opponents down. I follow their tactic to get the upper hand and aim for their manhood. I can't help but wince as I knee them in that spot, and they slump down on the ground in pain.

I can't blame them. It must really hurt. But for victory, I must continue doing it.

'There's not many of them left and I don't have a lot of bullets left,' Laya yells beside me. 'If we want to finish this off quicker before another storm of army officers arrives, we'll all have to work together to bring them down.'

'We can do this!' Indra yells back with a lot of enthusiasm. Yet, there is a hint of fear in his voice.

The rest nod their heads in agreement and I mumble to myself as a momentary distraction from this current scene, 'That seems like the best option.'

There are only five of them left and five of us in total. But if we're doing this together, they'll be tackled down in no time. I signal to Faye about the man in front of me charging towards us. She nods. The man doesn't slow down as he nearly approaches me. We take this as an opportunity. Faye brings out her leg and he topples down. We punch him for good measure, knocking him completely unconscious.

We look at each other, eyes wide in disbelief that we managed to do that. But it is short lived, as he yanks Faye down. I take a step closer, and he yells in alarm, 'Step any closer and I will choke her to death.'

'Calm down, man. Are you sure you want to do that though?' I ask calmly even though I actually want to run at him and knock him down.

I slowly take a step forward, and he immediately yells out, 'I said step back!'

I put my hands up in surrender. 'Okay, man. You need to chill out for a bit.'

The man is about to say something when he closes his eyes and slumps to the floor.

I gasp. 'What?'

'Aeni, we have no time to be making conversations with one of them,' Laya looks pissed off as she reprimands me. 'Come on!'

I turn to see that all of the army officers who were waiting for us at the station are slumped on the floor, some are unconscious and some are pretending for fear of getting killed. I thought they would be more well prepared and well trained but I guess they must have been slacking off, since we arrived as a surprise. Or maybe I can question the potential and quality of our army officers because they can definitely do better.

'Where do we go now?' Faye asks, wincing as she hugs her arm closer to her body.

'We have to find a car that will take us there,' Laya points to the gate that reaches the sky. The closer I take a look at it, the more massive it gets.

No one talks anymore and no more questions are being fired as we walk out of the station in silence. The silence doesn't continue for long, as we soon spot a vehicle parked just outside in the centre of the road. I spot the name on the back of the car—it is an SUV, that must be the name of the car I presume, since I know nothing about cars.

'I'll volunteer to drive since I'm sure that none of you know how to.' Laya heads to the driver's seat.

Nihal rushes to the front passenger seat and hollers, 'Holy my . . . this is amazing! We're riding in a car!'

I walk dejectedly and open the back door. I stare inside the car when Faye nudges me to go in. I sit down in the middle of the back seat, sandwiched between Indra and Faye.

Laya revs up the engine and it roars to life. Indra turns back to look at us. 'Do you guys believe we just did that? It was crazy! I mean, seriously did we just get out of that unscathed?'

'Not exactly unscathed,' Faye winces as she cradles her right arm, which still hurts and is looking way worse. I try to inspect it and it hangs in an awkward position. We can just tell by the look of it, her arm is definitely broken.

'Oh my god, Faye! Are you okay? Does it hurt that bad? What should we do?' Nihal grabs her broken arm.

She screams, 'Nihal! It hurts! Now you're just bloody making it all worse.'

I was going to warn Nihal, but I'm certain her scream does it. He looks guilty as he bites his nails, his way of trying to keep his calm in a high-stress situation. 'That needs to be treated. Like immediately,' I say.

'You think I don't know that?' Faye's concentrating on her broken arm and looks close to tears. 'I can't even feel my fingers, I can't move them. Hell, I can't even feel it anymore. My arm feels like it has already been detached from its socket.'

I calm her down, 'Take a deep breath. Calm down and don't think too much of the pain.'

'Shut up! Everyone just shut their mouth! You guys are just making everything worse!' Faye snaps, no doubt from the anger and pain consuming her. If she wasn't angry and annoyed with us right now, I'd find that even more worrisome.

I try again because I'm the closest to her and both Indra and Faye are looking at me helplessly as though I'm the only one who can find the solution to the situation. *But when has it ever not been that way?*

I try again, 'Faye, when did you get hurt? Because when I was fighting off the last guy who was still standing, you looked fine. So, when did this happen?' I point to her broken arm.

After a few moments, she says, 'When we were almost out of the station, one of them attacked me. You guys didn't see because everyone was dying to get out of there. So was I. But in my hurry, I didn't see him aiming at me. I don't want to talk about this anymore. The fact is, it's already broken. There's nothing we can do about it anymore. It probably has to be cut off.'

'Hey,' Indra says softly, 'don't say that. We'll do whatever it takes to get your arm back to normal. We've been through a lot of hurdles together, and this is just one more. I assure you that everything is going to be okay. Your arm too. We'll get through it all.'

The speech is somehow dedicated to all of us, and without realizing, it has lifted my spirits a bit and given me some hope.

I ask her again, 'Are you sure you're okay? I'll try and see what I can do.'

I try to mend her arm by wrapping it in a gauze, but I don't think it's doing her any good.

When I first took a glimpse of Faye's broken arm, I was so sure that it was too far away to salvage. Seeing it now, wrapped snugly against her body, I will myself to remain hopeful. Her broken arm will get better, she will get better, and we will all be fine in time.

# Chapter 27

'Is that an infirmary over there?' Nihal asks with great anticipation. He's been consistently asking if all the buildings we have encountered and passed by are infirmaries and they all turn out not to be. There aren't a lot of buildings here but he still remains hopeful that one of them might be an infirmary and not just an abandoned one.

'No, I don't think so,' I say as I take a closer look at it. I don't even know what I'm trying to look out for because even back on the Central Island, I rarely ever go to the infirmary. I've just seen it from a distance, five storey high and a building like none other, as it is covered all in white with only the word 'infirmary' plastered on the top for all to see.

'It's been hours already, and we haven't even found one!' Nihal complains, 'It'll get dark soon!'

'Hey! We're trying our best here! Just stop complaining!' Laya has had enough of him and I don't blame her. Even I'm getting tired of hearing him complain about it the past couple of hours.

'Whatever!'

'Where am I? Where are we?' Faye asks groggily at the back as she stirs awake.

Nihal assures her, 'Hey, don't worry about it, okay? We're going to get help for your arm.'

Faye looks like she's already given up. 'Aren't we supposed to be heading out of the island? What are we doing? No, stop this. It's useless to go look for an infirmary now! We'll jeopardize the plan. We need to get out of here!'

'Faye, you need to get treated. You—'

'No!' she snaps. 'This is not something that can be negotiated. We are getting out of this island, forget about my arm. Our lives are at stake here! Our lives are more important than an arm. Even if it is truly broken, I still have my left arm. But if we lose our lives, then we're gone forever.'

I turn around to look at her, 'Are you sure about this?'

'Yes, I am sure!' But her face doesn't say that she is sure. There may be a hint of uncertainty there.

'Faye, I know you're worried about us but you need to worry about yourself too. Your arm really needs to get treated right now,' Nihal persuades her.

'Nihal, can you just sit back and shut up right now? You're not helping at all.' She pushes him aside so that she can have a good view of the road ahead. 'Laya, drive towards the gate and don't stop or slow down. Even if one of these knuckleheads tell you to turn around and head somewhere else like the infirmary, do not stray away from the gate. Do you hear me?'

Laya raises an eyebrow and complies, 'If you say so.'

'Guys,' Indra starts, 'I'm not sure if you have realized this but we have company behind us.'

We all turn around to look, except for Laya, who is looking in the rear-view mirror. We remain quiet as we stare at whatever is waiting behind us when Faye finally interrupts the silence, 'We are in deep trouble now.'

A row of lights coming from an uncountable number of vehicles—trucks, cars, and even a tank—are trailing behind us like taillights.

'What should we do?' Faye whispers.

I say quickly and urgently, 'Speed up. Step on the gas pedal harder and the fastest this car can go and get the hell away from them!'

'I was thinking of doing exactly that.' Laya starts driving confidently and the vehicle vrooms. In that moment, she really does look fearless. I don't know if that's just how she really is or the royal blood in her, but I must admit that she is truly badass.

'Stop the vehicle!'

A voice blasts from the front of the enemy's vehicle, and the distance between our vehicles is only a few inches. It is a man's commanding voice, but Laya refuses to comply as she steps on the gas pedal until as far as it can go and whispers to herself, 'Like hell am I going to stop.'

'I command you to stop the vehicle right now!'

'That's not happening,' Laya whispers, but this time everyone in the vehicle can hear what she said, which is the point of it.

The vehicle goes as fast as it possibly can, and I grip my seat for dear life. Laya has managed to put a little more distance between us and our enemies than before. To our right, the gate is looming taller the faster we go.

As the gate gets closer, our hope blooms in wonder. But just then, a vehicle crashes into us. Our car skids round and round, making me dizzy, and I manage to catch a glimpse of another car crashing into us before everything goes dark and quiet.

* * *

I wake up with a start. My body is numb with pain, and it stings everywhere even when I move an inch. I'm sitting on the cold floor, my head leaning against the wall for support.

'OPEN THE DOOR!'

The light that is shining down on me is so bright, I see dots clouding my vision. I take a few more seconds before I open my eyes again. This time, the pieces and parts turn into one whole picture. Indra is sitting closest to me, and he's staring at the floor, his face hopeless as though he has given up on this life. Laya is pacing the room, and I assume she must be thinking of ways to get us out of this bolted room.

'OPEN THE DOOR! LET US OUT!'

Nihal is slamming against the door, screaming repeatedly and demanding attention from whoever is outside to release us.

'Where are we?' I ask groggily. My throat feels like sandpaper as I try to recall when was the last time I had a sip of water. I cannot even remember. It has been such a long time and the desire for even a drop of water is coursing through my mind and my stomach.

'You're up,' Indra comes closer to me. 'Where do you think we are?'

'Can you please not answer my question with another question?' I rub my temples to soothe my headache and try to make sense of my surroundings. Did I pass out?

'LET US OUT! LET US SEE HER!'

Words start to make sense, and I finally process what Nihal is screaming about. I look around for Faye, but she is nowhere to be found. I gesture for Indra to help me up even though my body is begging for me to sit still. Immediately, the room seems to spin.

'Where's Faye?' I ask, still rubbing my temple and blinking fast to make sense of my surroundings.

Indra looks despondent. 'She was taken away when she was screaming in pain and fainted on the ground. We don't know where they took her.'

I start to panic. 'What? They took her away?' I process what he said. 'Wait, what happened after our vehicle crashed?'

Leaning by the side of the room, Laya calmly says, 'Obviously, their plan worked. They got us by jamming our car between two vehicles on our right and left. Ugh!' She murmurs the last part to herself.

Laya's words spur Indra into action, and he pushes Nihal aside, continuing to rattle the door.

'Stop it. They won't open the door. You might as well just give up.' Laya grumbles in response.

I start making my deductions, trying to connect the dots. 'Are they the Permaisuri's men?'

Nihal shrugs. 'We're not su—'

'Of course, they are hers. Who else would it be? Who else has that kind of power to capture a bunch of teenagers on the loose? She's the only one! The only one who has done this and the only one who has an army of men at her beck and call!' Laya cuts in, enraged.

I get why she's angry and partially why she's pacing around like it'll solve all our problems.

'I don't think it is her. I have a feeling deep inside me that they're not her men,' I say what I have been keeping inside me.

'What are you talking about? You cannot be serious, are you, Aeni?' Laya gives me an uncertain look.

I put together my suspicions, 'I am. These men act so brash, like they don't have a care in the world, as though the orders they have received from the people above them have made the order in a split second—without calculating the consequences. Just try to remember—first of all, the Permaisuri has no idea why we're on the run—'

'She could just be turning a blind eye, haven't you heard of that?' Laya interrupts the moment she hears something about her sister.

I brush off her comment. 'Forget that. Second of all, things just don't add up.'

Laya laughs, desolate. 'The fact that you just have a feeling deep inside you and that things don't add up makes you suspicious about the people who have captured us not being the Permaisuri's men? Well, I don't know about you but it doesn't convince me. At all! You're just speaking nonsense.'

'Why do you hate her so much? What did she do to you that has made you so angry even at the mention of her name?' I wonder out loud.

'BECAUSE SHE KILLED MY PARENTS!'

Everyone is startled by Laya's outburst, even Nihal whose hand is now hanging in midair, his mouth open in surprise at her sudden revelation. No one looks directly at her, as if she hasn't said those words, as if suddenly the conversation never veered off in that direction.

She sighs and lightly bangs her head against the wall repeatedly. No one stops her, no one even dares to. Everyone is lost in their own thoughts and silence falls over the room. Even Indra has stopped rapping on the door, hands ruffling his mop of hair, and slumps dutifully on the floor, looking lost and dejected.

My mind wanders to a day when we were fifteen, making our way to the hill. Life was normal back then, we weren't being chased for something we didn't do, we hadn't met the Permaisuri and Laya. We hadn't left the Central Island, the one we call home. Sun was streaming down our faces. The clouds were a variety of shapes and sizes as they covered up the orange sky. It was a good day and nothing else mattered to us.

We hung out around the hill until the sun was setting, and it was time to return home. We spent hours talking about everything that came to our minds, playing games that we'd invented on our own while soaking in the evening sun. Now, that memory seems like a hazy dream in a nightmare full of monsters, lies, and deceit.

I hear footsteps. They stop just outside the door. Nihal is on his feet in minutes, waiting and hoping they'll let us go. The rest of us don't so much as move. Keys rattle just outside the heavy metal door. It opens wide, and a moment later, a man steps into the room—a dungeon or a jail would be a better description.

'Where's Faye? What have you done with her? Let us go! Release us, we have done nothing wrong!' Nihal says it all in one breath and tries to stand taller than the bulking man with biceps, his veins protruding where his clothes don't cover them.

The man who just entered is huge. He stands a head taller than Nihal. Even with sunglasses on, everyone can tell that he's giving Nihal a menacing look. He steps closer towards Nihal and crouches down so that they're looking face to face at each other before Nihal finally recoils from his combative gaze, wanting nothing to do with this man.

His voice is hoarse, yet it could probably be heard all the way from the edge of the island. 'Up, all of you! We're going to meet with the master!'

# PART V

## Chapter 28

He guides us up a winding staircase and through a long corridor, voices and sounds can be heard from every room that we pass by. No one questions him about where we're heading or who the master is. Everyone is being obedient, as no one wants to be smothered in his strong and tight grip that is also known to be his own form of torture.

After winding our way towards where the big guy claims we are to meet with the 'master', we finally stop in front of a double door that is made of pure brass. Well, whoever this master is, he's already taking precautions against danger. People like him are definitely the bad guys, right?

'You may step through. The master is waiting for you.'

We step into the room hesitantly to ensure that no one ambushes us. You never know, I'm just being extra cautious as I should be when meeting with the enemy.

The room is huge, approximately the size of three domiciles. The ceiling is high and a chandelier hangs in the middle that illuminates the whole room.

The chandelier has effortlessly made the whole room more extravagant and fancier. *That must be the master's taste, I suppose.* In the centre of the room, a man is sitting on what I presume to be his throne. He is casually sprawled across it, one leg on the throne that could actually fit three people.

'There you are, my fellow fugitives!' He stands up and gives us a warm smile. There's nothing warm about him at all despite his entrancing looks. I shiver in disgust as the man's features click. *It's Rat Guy.*

'Where's Faye? WHAT HAVE YOU DONE TO HER?' Nihal is the first to talk in the presence of the man in front of us.

Rat Guy tsks and smirks, 'Is that how they teach you to greet someone back at the Academy? That's not very nice. Let me show you a proper greeting for someone, especially for someone who is older than you are. Watch and listen to me carefully, I do not wish to repeat myself. First, you have to bow as an act of courtesy and give the best smile you can. A sincere one, not like you're seeing a monster. Do you think the person you greet would feel that it is coming from the bottom of your heart?'

No one answers him and he continues, 'Am I talking to myself here?'

Silence again.

He nods at someone behind us, 'Buva. Make them talk.'

The big guy whose name is Buva lifts me up with the back of my shirt like a doll, and I yelp. I move my arms and legs in protest, 'Let me go! Put me down!'

He looks smug. 'Now, let me try it again. Am I talking to myself here?'

I spit in his direction and yet, I still remain silent while squirming for Buva to put me down. The man nods again at Buva, who lifts Nihal with his other hand. What is this guy made of? Steel?

'Alas, children follow their parents' behaviour.' Rat Guy looks disgusted as he says, 'Let me repeat this again, and if you still refuse to do as I say, I will harm your other friend over there!' His face is pure murderous as he glances at the corner of the room and we follow his gaze. Faye is sitting there, her hands tied in a metal rope behind her back.

'NO!' Nihal screams out beside me, trying to get away from Buva's grasp. 'You're not talking to yourself! We're here listening to you. Please don't harm her. She has done nothing wrong. We beg you.'

'That's what I'm talking about. Now, do you know the reason why you're all here?' Rat Guy cackles with laughter.

I squirm again but Buva has a very tight grip on both of us. Seriously, how does he live and what does he eat to have a body that big and strong? Pure steel for all his meals?

'Let us go first!' I demand.

Rat Guy chuckles. 'What's the magic word, Aeni?'

I roll my eyes, voice mocking, 'Please?'

He claps and nods at Buva, who finally lets us down to the ground but not so gently.

'A bit more assurance in your pleas next time, yes?' Rat Guy demands.

I ignore his question.

'What do you want from us?' Laya says in a commanding voice. She cuts to the chase.

'What do I want from all of you?' Rat Guy pretends to think, humming and hawing. 'What do you think? I don't want that I'm the only one talking here, let there be a two-way communication in our discussion. It'll make the conversation much more interesting. How does that sound?'

'Sounds good,' I grumble when I see that no one else wants to take part in this stupid and ridiculous conversation. It honestly feels like I am actually talking to a child who is relentlessly trying to demand attention from the people around him. Rat Guy has always been full of himself, and I'm sick of it.

I scan the room, looking for a way to escape and get out of here, but every exit is being blocked by a military officer and Rat Guy's men, a mixture of both. How has he made some of the military officers working for the Permaisuri to turn against her?

I still have no idea what his motive behind capturing us is.

'Let me officially start the conversation,' I say and he looks excited. 'What do you want from us? What is your motive? Why do you have the Permaisuri's guards working with you?'

Rat Guy has the audacity to look amused. 'Wow! Aeni, I really appreciate your enthusiasm but you need to calm down and slow down your questions. I know you're getting excited there but if you could kindly ask me the questions one by one, that would be much better for both you and me.'

I eye him with suspicion. I have long forgone any respect for him, and now I just feel annoyed. 'Who are you, really? Are you our instructor from the Academy or are you just hiding behind a mask?'

'I am flattered that you finally asked me that question. I have been waiting for it. I know you have a brain somewhere inside you that will finally be put to use.' Rat Guy paces around his so-called throne. He clicks his tongue before continuing, 'Let me officially introduce myself. My name is Vikor, and I am the leader of this rebel group called Avlaeca. My father started it, and now I am taking over, officially beginning what my father planned but never did. He's just a coward, if you ask me. See, we have come to a conclusion and have a vision that the monarchy must be abolished. We must simply let the people of Killen decide. We have decided that the royal family does the people no good. We're living in the thirty-first century, for goodness' sake. We must be better than the past. Haven't you learned enough from the past to not have it repeat?'

Laya takes a step forward and stops at the foot of the baby stairs that lead up to the throne. 'I don't know if you have learned anything about Killen's history before, but we have lived in peace for the past seventy years! No wars raging in our city, no missiles flying in the sky, and no nonsense whatsoever of mass shootings.'

'Seventy years?' Vikor laughs sarcastically, 'How could you even compare that with two millennia? Haven't you learned history before?' He repeats the question again for Laya.

She stands by her stance. 'Forget about history, let's just talk about the present. There have been no major crimes, like murders or arson, ever since Killen was first established. The biggest crime the citizens have tried committing is running away and that only involves themselves and no one else around them. Does that count as nothing to you? Does that not sound like peace to you?'

Rat Guy looks smug. 'Why are you defending the monarchy so much? Aren't you on the brink of escaping from Killen to leave everything behind?' He pauses. 'Especially your sister, Mahsuri?'

Laya looks annoyed at the mention of her sister. 'What has she got to do with this conversation?'

'Oh, she has everything to do with this conversation and my plans for her in the future, including the people and the entirety of our beloved city, Killen. It will be a blast for everyone but more so for me. Don't you just feel giddy hearing that? I know I do!'

'You're crazy. I bet you don't hear people telling you that every day. So, let me say it again, you are freaking crazy!' Laya spits out angrily.

'Don't worry, I have heard that phrase being thrown at me on certain occasions in the past. Can't say that I liked it. It was a dark time for me, yes.'

'Why are you capturing us and locking us away in the dungeon? What have we done to you to be treated this way?' I butt in.

'That's easy. The four of you have resisted my serum, which was brilliantly formulated by yours truly. How is it only the four of you have managed to resist it? I turned everyone static and still using the exact same serum? I'm sure you have encountered that already. I had to inject them with the serum once again, thanks to the four of you for making my work more complicated than it already is but you still resisted. Why is that? What kind of special powers do you have that I am simply not aware of?'

The shock is palpable but I don't let it show that his words have fazed me. Knowing from past encounters with the man, his ego will be bruised when his words don't have the ability to placate me.

'That's easy,' I repeat his words from before, 'because we know the truth.'

'It can't be. That can't be.' He shakes his head. 'What have I missed? What must I do to make it work?'

'We get it, your serum didn't work on us! Could you let me go now? This posture is killing me! How about some mercy?' Faye yells from the corner of the room and is looking very much annoyed by it.

I continue her argument, 'How about you just let us go and let us be on our freaking way? How does that sound to you? So, your stupid serum didn't work on us? That would be your fault and not ours. So, why don't you let us go?'

'I need to think. I must think.' Vikor paces around us. 'That's impossible. How can that happen? I have done a thousand tests and trials and they have all succeeded without a hitch.'

'Maybe the universe is just against you and your evil plans with your stupid little group,' Nihal says. 'And also can you release her already?'

'Hey, you! Some equality around here would be really nice,' Faye yells at both Buva and Vikor, who looks at her briefly before looking away and sitting down. He murmurs, 'How did this happen?'

'Woohoo! Hello? I am tied down here!' Faye says again.

Vikor rolls his eyes and utters agitatedly to his loyal companion, guard, friend, or whoever he is to Vikor, 'Release her. I cannot think if she says one more word.'

Buva releases Faye, and she rushes towards us and Nihal is the first to reach her. Indra and I follow closely behind him. Nihal immediately checks for any sign of injuries or assault. He inhales shocked, 'Your arm? How—'

I, too, am shocked by the state of her arm.

'They healed me. It's all fine now. They did something to my arm while I was out of it, and it's all fine now.' She caresses her right arm lovingly and gives Nihal a small smile. 'Just like you said it would.'

'You heard me?' He looks ashamed yet glad to hear it.

'I did.'

'Enough!' Vikor bellows, 'You're not in some soap drama, for goodness' sake. We have more important matters to talk about if everyone is ready to hear it.'

'About time,' Indra says sarcastically.

'Don't be smart with me! I don't like it. You will just piss me off and I will have to send you back to your dungeons. So, stop cutting me off when I'm talking here! I swear, you people just have no manners and you should be ashamed of yourselves.'

'Okay, we get it,' Indra holds his arms up defensively, as if surrendering. He rolls his eyes at me. I have to agree it is as though Vikor's mental age doesn't corelate with his actual age. He's so childish—an adult ganging up on a bunch of teenagers.

'Now,' Vikor starts speaking while walking down the stairs, 'you know about my plans. I have no choice but to terminate all of you.'

He stops right in front of Laya. 'Especially you.'

He laughs evilly and chills run down my spine. This guy is definitely not sane.

# Chapter 29

'You can't do this to us! This is madness!' Nihal protests.

Indra tries to reason. 'Let me talk to Vikor again! Let me persuade him!'

Nihal and Indra are the only ones who still have the motivation to protest and rebel as they relentlessly bang the door. The rest of us sit back in our own corners, deep in our own thoughts.

I'm thinking about what is going to happen now to the citizens back on the island. My ma. My friends' families. The Permaisuri. And everyone else.

'Guys, can we have some quiet here please?' I sigh.

'No!' they both reply, and Nihal continues, 'We can't just let him get away with this! He can't just terminate us if he wishes to. That guy is a criminal, he's the villain, and we must do everything in our power to fight him. I am not stopping.'

'Suit yourself,' Faye leans her head on the wall and closes her eyes. What happened to her? Where is the feisty fighting spirit of Faye that was so visible back there against Vikor? Where has that part of her gone? Why is she so full of contradictions? It's odd when I think about it.

'This is just madness,' Laya laughs to herself. 'It's just unbelievable to think that a man like that exists in Killen. He's basically worse than my sister.'

'You really hate her, don't you?' Faye asks, oblivious of how much Laya resents the Permaisuri. I can't blame her.

Laya ignores her and stands up instead, walking towards the door where Nihal and Indra are perched on the metal gate. 'You're right. We need to do something. We can't just let this happen. We have a purpose, and we must work towards it!'

'What plan do you have in mind?' I ask.

Laya smirks, 'I hope it'll get us out of here and knock someone down!'

'Yeah!' Nihal whoops.

Indra smirks, 'That's what I'm talking about!'

Faye is still leaning on the wall with her eyes closed and I'm not sure if I want to join in their excitement just yet. Of course, we have to figure out a way to get out of here and make our way off this island, but I'm just tired of fighting and thinking that we can beat down the bad guys all the time. Even though every time we have tried to kick them down, somehow miraculously, we have managed to make it out alive—painfully and with bruises all over our bodies, but alive nonetheless.

I sound like a coward right now, I know. You would be this way too if you were in my position.

'Aeni? What do you say about this? Are you in?' Nihal looks at me expectantly—all three of them do.

'Let's go with our original plan,' I say decisively.

'Faye?' Nihal asks.

She finally opens her eyes and sits up properly with a determined look on her face. 'I'm in.'

'Okay, we've got one thing settled, and we have all agreed on this.' Nihal looks at each of us. 'What do we do now?'

'If someone says "we plan" one more time . . . I'm out,' I joke to lighten the mood, but no one seems into it.

'Let's just bust out of here,' Laya suggests and her two loyal followers nod their heads in agreement. She continues, 'Here is what I have come up with—we'll yell and wait for someone to come and open the door. We can all yell to show them how urgent the situation is. When we're out, we will head down to where that Vikor is, and I'll be the one to kill him. We'll make our way out of here, steal one of their vehicles, and get to the gate and off the island. Is the plan clear?'

'Kill him?'

'Wait, who said anything about killing anyone?'

The loyal followers start to protest the idea.

'You want to kill him?' I add before Laya says anything.

'Yes,' she says bluntly, seemingly without realizing that her plan could eventually take a toll on each and every one of us in this room. 'Laya, you need to think it all through. Killing does not have to be a part of the plan. It wasn't even a part of the original plan—'

'Well, the original plan didn't include a psycho man who is intending to bring chaos and create a fiasco in all of Killen. The original plan was just to get the hell out of this island and leave everything behind. But now things have changed and when that happens, there will always be room to improvise.'

'You will be a murderer, a killer, and whatever else that title entitles you with,' I'm trying to make a point but I doubt it's bringing any effect to the situation right now, 'Killing doesn't always solve the problem. It'll only worsen the problem and that's what has happened in the past. You'll only be repeating mistakes that have already been sealed and done.'

'You may be thinking this in my point of view but you're forgetting about the major points of view. Our island, the people and . . . Permaisuri.'

She was hesitating to include her sister in the conversation but there's no uncertainty there that she actually, truly cares about her. Well, you know what they say, blood runs thicker than water no matter how hard we try to get as far away as we can from our family members, they'll always be a part of us, a part of who we are and what we're made of.

'And our families,' Indra adds, 'what will happen to them if we just let Rat Guy on the loose while we have a clear evidence right in front of us that he has insane and ludicrous plans for them. Even if we somehow manage to get out of this city, one thing for sure is that our families will be okay. That's the most important thing.'

Laya nods. 'We have to kill a tainted man so he does not taint our society. That's the only purpose of this plan. I hope you understand my intention and motive behind having this purpose because if you do not wish to take this stand with me, you are more than welcome to go first. I am capable of taking care of this on my own.'

'No!' Faye is confident about her choice. It's written all over her face as she says the next words, 'I'm in this. It will be a cause with a meaning and I will not back down from it. If they wish to cut my hand this time, that's fine with me. I still have my other hand and my other body parts I can live with.'

'Do you really mean that?' Nihal asks and she nods while focusing her gaze on the girl with the big plan—Laya.

Indra takes a step forward, 'Then I'm in too. I cannot bear the idea that something bad could happen to my family when I'm out there. Even my little brother, no matter how annoying he can be.'

'I'm in too,' I say and I don't add my explanation like the two just did. *It's enough, right?*

Suddenly, the door to our dungeon is unbolted. Wordlessly, all of us, except for Faye who has her arms around her torso, act.

'What is going on here?' It is another one of Vikor's oblivious followers. He scans the room to figure out why we are causing so much noise. He isn't given the opportunity to question us further and to even wonder what is going on as Indra elbows him right between his eyes and as if that wasn't enough, Laya knees his crotch. It doesn't take long for him to come tumbling down to the ground.

# Chapter 30

'Let's move!' Laya announces.

She leads the whole way back to what I assume is the throne room and we don't stop even when we have reached our destination. All of us contribute to forcing the door open. Vikor takes a few moments before he finally acknowledges our presence. 'Shouldn't all of you be locked up in the dungeon? What are you doing here?'

He neither looks surprised nor angry to see us barging in. He stays unfazed and expressionless. It's hard to read what he is actually thinking.

'Aren't you glad to see us here?' Nihal says sarcastically.

'I can't say I am glad per se but I can say that I might have underestimated all of you for a bit. I didn't get the impression that you were fighters. I didn't expect it at all.' He stands up, walks towards us, down the stairs, and stops short as if deliberating. 'Now what should I do with the lot of you?'

'I suggest you just let us go,' Laya commands, coming straight to the point, her tone full of authority.

Vikor circles around us. 'I cannot do that. That would be my loss then. All my efforts and fortuitous acts will have been for nothing. Letting all you go would make my plan be for naught.' He looks around for Buva, but his buddy is not here. That's when he starts to panic but quickly masks it.

'Now, where is Buva? I thought he was just here a moment ago.' Vikor puts his hands together and beams. 'Alas, we shall move on to more pressing matters. Why do you wish—no why do you even simply have the idea of getting out of our city? It does not make sense to me. Don't you realize how safe we are in here with no war ravaging everything? Our city is nothing but peaceful at the moment. Although I cannot guarantee that much longer, since I am the head of this rebellion against the monarchy. Wait, does that make me the bad guy here or what?'

I finally speak up, getting tired of this fool with an ego as high as a mountain. 'Just let us go quietly and we won't cause you more trouble than we already have.'

'If you say so. When you get outside there, don't say that I didn't tell you so because I did.' He's not looking at us when he says those words while playing with his cuff.

'Enough! We have no time for this. We should just act now before one of his backups arrive,' Laya says with conviction. Now, we are all just waiting for one of us to act first before actually moving on with the plan—kill Vikor, ending him once and for all.

'Act? What have you been planning without me?' Vikor pretends to feel hurt.

'What makes you think we're going to tell you anything?' Indra taunts him.

'Sounds intriguing. I look forward to it.' Vikor turns around and climbs up the stairs before sitting down on the throne. He looks up, this time looking impatient. 'Now, stop wasting my time.' He looks around, 'Where is Buva when I need him?'

Both Faye and Laya advance towards Vikor who no longer looks smug and actually seems nervous about the turn of events. Faye gets to him first and hesitates a little before she has her arms wrapped around his neck. Faye is acting as though whoever reaches Vikor first wins the upper hand. I frown, wondering why she's acting that way. For all we know, we're all on the same team, with the same goal in our minds.

'Ah, Ms Li. What a turn of events. Are you no longer working for me? Have you pledged your allegiance to these fools instead? I'm hurt.' Vikor laughs vibrantly, and he actually has the decency to be amused by the situation.

The shock is evident on our faces. The three of us feel betrayed. Laya seems unfazed by Vikor's words and continues to tighten her grip on him. So all this while, the reason why Faye has not been herself, constantly challenging us and making us do the opposite of what we think is the better path to take, has been because of this? She has been working for the rebellion?

I feel like cowering away but once I process his words again, anger boils and I am the first to vent it out, 'Faye, is that true?' I want to add more but my voice shakes and that's all I manage to say.

Indra remains silent, and Nihal slumps on the floor, eyes glued to the ground. 'So, all this while, you were a spy? A double agent for . . . for this man with his stupid plans?' His voice gradually gets louder and is laced with fury.

Faye refuses to look at us and instead focuses on Vikor. 'You just shut your mouth!' Faye has him in a tighter grasp but the smile on Vikor's face does not fade away.

'Do you actually think you can defeat me? Me? The master of Avlaeca? The great Vikor? I would like to see you try.' The smug look on his face is back. He adds, curious now, 'How are you even going to kill me without any weapon in your hands? After all, you are just a bunch of kids and it's pitiful!'

'You forget that our hands are a weapon on their own,' Laya says proudly.

He gasps in mock surprise. 'How fascinating.'

Laya cuts to the chase, 'Finish him off.'

'Wait!' Vikor cuts her off but a sound interrupts him. It's coming from outside. We stare at the door that is wide open, heading towards the corridor. A screeching sound can be heard even from miles away, and I have to cover my ears, not wanting to hear the disturbing sound.

'Is that. . .' Nihal whispers, not believing his eyes.

I look up and a figure is slowly making her way over here. The cape is bellowing in the wind with her long hair swishing from side to side. Her stride is confident, and it seems like nothing can bring her down.

I can't believe it. It's her. It really is the Permaisuri.

Laya grimaces. 'What the hell is she doing here?'

She stops at the doorway and Vikor gasps, 'Mahsuri?'

The Permaisuri's face comes into the light. 'Long time no see, Vikor.'

Vikor tries to get out of Faye's hold, but she refuses to let him get away from her death grip. He begs, 'Let me go!'

'In your dreams.' Permaisuri continues walking towards us. Everyone is holding their breaths as we try to anticipate her next move.

Vikor tries to free himself yet again. But this time, Indra moves to help Laya keep him at bay, adding, 'Don't even think about going anywhere.'

Permaisuri stops short right in front of Vikor. She grabs his collar. 'What are you still doing here?'

He tries to laugh. 'Mahsuri, aren't we friends? Is this any way to greet an old friend? You wound me deeply.'

'I have demoted you to be an Academy instructor in the hopes that you will atone for your past mistakes. Why are you still doing this?'

'My dear, I have never, not once, dropped my big plans. I have been lying low, waiting for the right time to take action again. I have waited years for this exact moment.'

Laya steps in, 'Look, you're just wasting your time. We have everything under control. You should leave.'

'My sister, are you really this naïve?' the Permaisuri lets go of Vikor and swivels her gaze to Laya. 'Killen is my city to govern, and I will not let anyone try to destroy it. I know better than that.'

The Permaisuri turns around to stare at the chamber and even makes eye contact with me. But I don't dare to keep looking at her and look elsewhere instead. 'Besides,' she adds, 'I may be the best person to deal with Vikor here. Me and him, we go way back.'

'Wait a minute there, I think I deserve more credit than that. Yes, we do go way back but the least I could get is more than that. Fine, if you won't tell her then I will. Laya, you may not remember me, but I used to be the Permaisuri's trusted general.' Vikor looks hurt that Permaisuri isn't giving him credit where it is due.

*What?* I did not expect that.

Laya gives him a blank look. 'I won't be able to remember someone as insignificant as you. Actually, I don't even want to.'

'I trusted you, Vikor, but you went behind my back! I even gave you a second chance in the past and I genuinely thought of you as a friend. But you took advantage of me and you have always been set on ruling over Killen by overthrowing me. To bring the monarchy down and let your foolish rebellion take over.' Even when the Permaisuri is mad, she remains poised and doesn't let emotions sway her. All her attention seems to be directed at Laya. She grabs Laya's arms to make Laya look her in the eyes, but Laya remains stubborn. The Permaisuri hesitates before speaking. 'Laya, I don't know how else I should tell you this but our parents . . . Vikor was the one who killed them.'

'WHAT?' Laya bellows, finally making eye contact with her sister and desperately searching for the truth.

The Permaisuri has been looking regal until now, but as she slumps to the floor, she just looks like someone who is grieving deeply. 'I'm sorry. I tried to tell you, but you never gave me the chance. I know I owe it to you to tell you the truth. I'm so sorry.'

Laya seethes, 'Then why is he still alive? Why did you still give him a chance? What kind of Permaisuri are you?' she pauses looking pained. 'No, what kind of a daughter are you? Ayahanda and Bonda would be so disappointed if they knew this is how you handled things. You don't deserve to rule the city.'

The Permaisuri looks heartbroken. 'I'm sorry. He was my only friend whom I trusted, and I was blinded then. I expelled him from Killen, but I didn't know he was back.' She tries to stand up again and looks to be struggling, so I help her up. 'No more. I will not spare him my mercy anymore. I owe it to you and to

Ayahanda and Bonda in the name of justice. All of you should leave. Right now!'

'What are you going to do?' Laya asks, eyes brimming with tears.

The Permaisuri smiles, tears running down her face. 'What he has deserved right from the very beginning. Leave now!'

I pull Nihal and Indra with me to hurry and leave the room. Laya and Faye walk hesitantly. Laya keeps looking back to where the Permaisuri is. I completely ignore Faye and think to myself, I will confront her later when the time is right.

# Chapter 31

We go down a flight of stairs until we reach the ground level. As our luck would have it, Buva is waiting downstairs. He appears to be rushing somewhere until he spots us. 'Wait, how did you get here?'

We immediately turn around to make a run for it but luck doesn't seem to be on our side. Faye is the closest to him, and he grabs her. 'You're not going anywhere, you little spy. I've got you now.' He holds her tightly in his arms.

I look around for a weapon. It will be totally impossible for me to bring him down given his size. I grab the first thing I see—a shattered glass bottle—and aim it at him. 'Let her go! You big man, let her go!'

Faye is still struggling in his grasp. Buva whispers in her ear with a devilish smile, 'How can you just betray us like that? We gave you a mission and you couldn't even keep your word. We are very disappointed in you. We truly are. Master had such high hopes from you and you just betrayed us like that. For that, you are going to pay.'

Faye seethes, 'I would rather die than work with someone like you and betray my friends.' She looks at each one of us, admitting defeat. She gives us a brave smile, as if to reassure us.

My mind is working hard to try and figure out how to get her out of Buva's grasp but nothing seems to be in our favour, even if we execute it.

He momentarily glances at me. 'Any last words for your friend, little girl?'

Faye shakes her head as I take a step forward, just me and the bottle against a giant who is seemingly unstoppable in combat.

Faye mouths the words, 'I'm sorry.'

Buva takes out a knife, holds it against her neck before slicing through it in one swift motion and letting her go. Faye slumps to the floor, her eyes wide open.

I scream, the sound reverberating through the entire building. Soon, I hear footsteps coming down the stairs.

Blood is already pooling on the floor, and my sight gets blurry as I hold my friend's lifeless body. I shake her, 'Faye? Faye! Wake up! Please, wake up! Faye Li, you better wake up right now!'

Nihal takes one look at Faye before immediately walking away to catch the culprit. 'You!' He tries to do some damage, but Buva is just too strong for him. Nihal is on the ground now, but he still refuses to give up. He wipes the blood running down his nose. 'Come on! What are you waiting for? Kill me!'

Indra tries to pull him away and make him see sense but the Permaisuri is back. This time, with an entourage. She gestures to the person beside her and commands, 'Capture him.'

As I clutch Faye in my arms, I finally let it all go and shed my tears, hoping that my friend will miraculously come back to life. I try to check for a pulse but it's gone. *She's really gone.*

Indra comes to my side and embraces me. Nihal remains by the side. We make him join us as we cry together, grief enveloping us.

# Chapter 32

'You need to let her go now,' Indra says quietly as I refuse to let Faye's lifeless body go. The paramedics as well as the military are here. Some of them have bruises covering their faces, and they don't look our way, finally knowing whose side we're actually on.

Indra's voice is laced with pain, 'Let them handle this. Aeni, let her go.'

I let her go with a heavy heart. It pains me that not only did I misunderstand her but I also didn't get the chance to apologize. Our relationship had been rocky ever since this fiasco started. I can't look at the depressing scene as the paramedics take Faye away so I turn around.

Laya walks towards me and pats my shoulder. 'I'm sorry for your loss.'

Nihal looks forlornly when the paramedics cover Faye's body with a white cloth. Then, they walk away, taking her back to the Central Island.

The Permaisuri comes over. 'You are all pardoned. Your courage and bravery have helped defeat those who tried to destroy Killen. All of you have my highest regards. You may decide however you wish to proceed from now on. Whatever wish you may have will be granted be it to continue your journey outside the city or remain within. Just tell me your decision and I will make it happen.

'I want you to remember that you are heroes. Faye, too, was a hero.'

The Permaisuri walks away before stopping by her sister's side.

Laya nods at her.

'Will I see you at home?' The Permaisuri asks.

Laya shrugs. 'We'll see.'

Baby steps. Anything is possible, after all.

They linger in front of the building and the activity ceases as the paramedics have already taken all the bodies away. Even the military is almost done assessing the place and just four of them are left behind. Our group is now missing one person, and it already feels like there is a huge gap.

No one appears to say anything until Laya starts the conversation, 'What are you going to do now? Go back or continue on ahead?'

I make my decision. 'I'm going back. There's nothing for me out there in that wasteland. My home is here—in Killen.'

'Aeni's right. Our home is in Killen and right now, it needs us more than ever. We need to restore it back to its glory, especially the people and our families. The Permaisuri called us heroes and something needs to change now that she has us in her highest regard.'

Laya continues to stare at the wall that separates Killen from outside civilization. That is, if it even exists.

'I don't know. I still want to see for myself what's out there. There's not much tying me down here.'

'Whatever you decide, I hope you still consider us your friends,' I say.

She gives me a small smile and nods, genuinely looking touched.

Nihal assesses the building one last time and announces, 'We should head back. I want to go home.'

'Yeah, we should go,' Indra agrees.

I look at Laya. 'Are you coming?'

She ponders, 'Yeah, I think I have to sleep on it before I make a decision. Come on, I'd love to see the Central Island, which I've heard so much about.'

We get in a car left for us to drive back to the station. One of the military officers is sitting stoically as he sees us making our way over. Nihal calls shotgun and I take the middle seat, squished between Laya and Indra.

Both of them are intently looking into the distance, darkness still enveloping the vast land. A sob breaks out of Nihal but no one says anything. Throughout the ride, the only sound is the wind swooshing in from the open window. Before long, we reach our destination.

We board the train and everyone remains in their own corners, some may be replaying the events of the past few days or even the past few weeks that have led to the events that happened tonight, in remembrance to our friend who will be missed.

I must be too overcome with fatigue because my head lolls and I doze off, letting sleep take me away. My last view is of the wall that I hope to never come across again.

* * *

Indra shakes me. 'Wake up, Aeni. We're back on the Central Island.'

I look around the train, Indra and I are the only ones left inside. True enough, as we step outside into the fresh air, I know we've arrived back to the city that I have grown up in. We walk out of the station. Everything is silent, except for a few birds chirping around above.

'So, this is it. The Central Island!' Laya exclaims as she stares around the city—at the tall buildings of the Hub, the Academy to the left, and the river to the right. The tram is already in motion as it zooms past us to its destination, moving across the city.

'Yeah, this is it,' I say.

Nihal looks like he's about to collapse and Indra comes to his rescue. 'Aeni, I'm going to take him home.'

'Yeah, you should go,' I respond.

As they turn to leave, I stop them. Indra looks at me curiously. Without giving it a second thought, I embrace them. I try to comfort them through this action and hope it's enough.

I whisper, voice shaking, 'We will get through this. Faye will be so proud of us.'

Nihal clutches tighter, and we finally let go as Nihal starts to sway. I say, 'I'll see you later. Stay strong, guys. Love you!'

They walk away into the tram, leaving me with Laya. She is still gazing at the skyscrapers. I ask her, 'You okay there?'

She nods enthusiastically. 'I've never seen such a tall building before.'

I ask, 'So, what's your plan?'

I desperately want to go home and see Ma, but it would be rude to just leave her all alone.

She finally turns her attention to me. 'I want to look around.'

She must have caught my hidden message so she relents. 'Sorry to keep you. I'll be fine on my own. You can go now. Just tell me your domicile number, and I will find you later.'

I tell her and once she has reassured me that she'll be fine, I leave her to it. I don't feel like taking the tram. My house is just across the river so I take a breezy walk, relishing in the familiarity of my surroundings.

The city still has no signs of activity. No one is out and about. I wonder about it, but once I reach my row, I forget about it and rush into the house. I call out, 'Ma!'

The house is silent. I head straight to Ma's bedroom. There she is, sleeping on the bed peacefully. I try to wake her, hoping to hear her voice, which I've missed so much, but she remains unmoving.

The serum must still be in effect. The paramedics warned me that it will take some time to wear off. But soon, everything will return to normal.

I lie down beside her and snuggle, feeling like a child once again.

As I stare out at the sky, Ma stirs and murmurs, 'Hmm, Aeni.'

She says something else. It is all gibberish, but it's enough for me. I'm already content to be here, right where I'm supposed to be.

*I'm home.*

# Chapter 33

Things have started settling down. Yet, the events of weeks past remain hidden away at the back of our minds.

Laya never made it to my house. But, a few days ago, she visited and said she was going to explore outside, she was leaving the city. She said it was only going to be temporary. She wants to be the one to leave and come back to tell the tale. To quote her words, 'Don't miss me too much, and I'll come back to visit soon.'

Her relationship with her sister still seems to be tense but it has gotten better and could even be back to how it was before the misunderstanding between them.

I'll constantly be on the lookout for her and welcome her when she returns.

Our lives are slowly going back to normal—as normal as they can be—and we are finally graduating from the Tertiary Academy soon, just counting the days now. The Ministry of Education even announced a whole new system, wherein we will now have another aptitude test. It will not be totally based on the test. But after, we can decide for ourselves what we would like to do in our future. Then there will be a training period before we officially start working as functioning adults in society.

So many things have changed and it's for the better. I'm looking forward to a better Killen altogether.

Today is Faye's funeral. But funerals have never been a big thing here in the city. Just the burial and that's basically it. We have usually seen others losing loved ones from a distance. It seems to be the kind of emotion that I can't even begin to describe now that I've lost someone I love. Nihal, Indra, and I huddle together under the rain as they lower Faye's body into the ground and bury her.

We stay back after everyone has gone and the rain has stopped. We share our memories of Faye and try to keep our spirits up. But deep down, everyone knows just how much it pains us to have lost someone so dear.

We are definitely going to miss her so much for a very long time. Rest in peace, my friend. We will see you soon.

* * *

Time seems to be moving to the beat of its own drum. Graduation has come and gone. The day of my aptitude retest arrives. I leave the house feeling hopeful. After much deliberation, I have finally decided to work in the infirmary, just like Ma and

Faye. I want to save others' lives and live Faye's dream to commemorate her memory.

I'm walking home after a day of training. I finally understand what Ma feels all the time—tending to patients and making sure everything goes as planned through the hectic days at the infirmary.

Someone calls my name, 'Aeni!'

I turn around and it's Mr Li. He tries to muster a smile but quickly drops the idea. He just lost his only family. I cannot imagine how that must feel.

'Hi, Mr Li, what can I help you with?'

He shoves his hand inside his jacket and says, 'I've been meaning to give you this.'

He uncovers a letter and gives it to me, 'I know you'd like to read this. Faye wrote it before she left, you know, in case she . . . she didn't make it.'

His eyes fill with tears and I want to console him, but he quickly says, 'I'll be gone, serving the military again. I just want to say thank you for being Faye's friend. She had it tough, living without her mama, and I owe it to you, to all of you, for being there for her. Make sure you relay this to Nihal and Indra too. I wish you luck with all your endeavours, Aeni. Goodbye.'

He doesn't wait for my response and goes on his way. That would be the last time I ever see him.

I am awestruck all the way to the hill, where Indra and Nihal are already waiting for me. We agreed to meet there to watch the sunset together.

I trek up the hill and soon enough, I spot Indra, who is picking away at the leaves. Nihal is looking out into the distance.

Indra beams when he sees me. 'Aeni, you're here!'

'Here I am!' I wave. Nihal turns around and gives me a weak smile as a greeting.

Indra senses something is off about me and asks in concern, 'What is it? What's wrong?'

'On my way here, I met Mr Li and he gave me this.'

I show them the letter and Nihal is quick to react, coming over to inspect it, 'Isn't this Faye's handwriting?'

I nod. 'Should we read it together?'

Something seems to be caught in Nihal's throat as he says, 'Yeah.'

I unfold the letter and we start to read quietly.

I dedicate this letter to dad and my dear friends, Nihal, Aeni, and Indra.

I assume if you are reading this, I am no longer alive. I have prepared this letter in advance in case things don't work out in my favour. I would like to confess something I should have told you a long time ago. A few weeks ago, before the first doses of the serum were distributed, someone by the name Buva wanted me to work for their cause. Avlaeca, they call themselves. My job was to aid them by leading us astray, to not leave the Central Island until they get here. Buva threatened me to work with him. Otherwise, he would hurt the ones I love the most. I did what he wanted in the beginning, but I knew it was not the right thing to do. Anyway, you guys were too stubborn to fall for it anyway, and I applaud you for that. Tonight, we are leaving the city behind and they will call me a traitor, but I don't care. I may be weighed down with guilt, but deep down, I know I would never let the bond of our friendship break. Even if I have to make some men angry along the way, I'd gladly do it all over again. Finally, it feels like a weight has finally been lifted off my chest, and I can die with no regret.

Dad, I'm sorry for not being the daughter you wanted me to be and I'm sorry for constantly making things hard for you when I was growing up. But I'm so proud to be your daughter, and I love you with all my heart.

Indra, I know we don't spend much time together, but let's admit it, it's kind of awkward when it's just the two of us. But I'm still happy to have you as my friend.

Aeni, I know we aren't like all the other girlfriends at the Academy, but we cannot deny that we are just as awesome in our own way. You have been like an older sister as well as a mother figure to me throughout our growing up years. I do regret that we haven't spent more time together—just the two of us without the boys, just girls' time.

Nihal, I know we used to argue so much and I honestly never took any of the words you said to heart. Actually, I would sometimes replay all the silly arguments we had in the past. Start afresh, I know you can do it.

I love you all and please don't be too sad. You should live your own lives too, but don't forget me altogether. You are allowed to only remember me occasionally. Just know I'm not going anywhere and that I will always be here right beside you. Perhaps in the next life, I will look for you. There hasn't been a day when I haven't loved you. I do, I love you and I can't imagine having lived my life without you.

With love,
Faye Li

We fold the letter, processing our emotions as we watch the sun set, the long day finally replaced with darkness. We stay there for a long time before deciding it's finally time to head back to our respective homes, where our families will be waiting.

I look at the only friends I have left and am glad that I still have them. 'Should we go?'

Nihal nods in response.

With a dimpled smile, Indra says, 'I'll follow you both—wherever you go.'

# Acknowledgements

This book is a collaborative work between teenage Naadhira and adult Naadhira writing (2015), rewriting (2021), and editing (2024). It truly feels so surreal that a story I got as an idea for when I was sitting for my form 4 paper 2 maths exam is finally being published as a book ten years later. Now, don't come to me and ask me more about this, my family will be disappointed in me!

I'd really like to thank Nora Nazarene Abu Bakar for reaching out to me and somehow knowing my inner thoughts. It has always been one of my dreams to publish with Penguin SEA, and Alhamdulillah, I made it! If she had not reached out, this manuscript would have just been collecting dust on my laptop. Thank you for the opportunity to help me pursue what I had lost hope in years ago.

Thank you to the Penguin SEA team for working on my full-of-flaws manuscript and making it into something more readable.

To my Bookstagram fam for always being such a warm and supportive community. To my non-bookish friends, who don't get what I am up to most of the time but are still so encouraging. I love you, guys!

To my family for raising me to be the person I am today. I know it's a lot to ask, but I hope you are proud of me.

Finally, thank you to my readers for picking up my book. I hope it temporarily leads you to a better place than the harsh reality we live in today.